Anonymous

Methodism in a Nutshell

a plain and comprehensive view of the usages and doctrines of the

Methodist church, with an appendix

Anonymous

Methodism in a Nutshell
a plain and comprehensive view of the usages and doctrines of the Methodist church, with an appendix

ISBN/EAN: 9783337390792

Printed in Europe, USA, Canada, Australia, Japan

Cover: Foto ©Andreas Hilbeck / pixelio.de

More available books at **www.hansebooks.com**

Methodism in a Nutshell.

A

PLAIN AND COMPREHENSIVE VIEW OF
THE USAGES AND DOCTRINES OF
THE METHODIST CHURCH.

WITH AN APPENDIX.

P; a Member of the Tennessee Conference.

Nashville, Tenn.:
SOUTHERN METHODIST P   HING HOUSE.
PRINTED FOR THE AUTHOR.
1880.

PREFACE.

FEELING that there is a demand for a brief and comprehensive work containing the usages and doctrines of the Methodist Church, we have endeavored to satisfy it by producing the following work. The author claims no originality, although he may not have given the names of the authors when he quoted their language. Hoping that our book will meet the existing demand, and be useful and do good, we submit it to an intelligent and indulgent public.

THE AUTHOR.

ALEXANDRIA, TENN., Oct. 1, 1879.

CONTENTS.

6   *Contents.*

Contents. 7

METHODISM IN A NUTSHELL.

CHAPTER I.

ORIGIN AND PROGRESS.

JESUS CHRIST gave the commission, "Go ye therefore, and teach all nations;" and some say his disciple, Simon, crossed over into Great Britain, in A.D. 35, and there preached the gospel.

The Church contended against heathenism during the eight centuries prior to her earnest contentions against Romanism. St. Augustin, in the fourth century, found the Church scattered by persecution. From the eighth to the fourteenth century she struggled hard, and to some extent successfully, against Romanism.

Wycliffe's publications and the blood of the martyrs were the seed of the Reformation, for which we are indebted to Luther, Cranmer, Latimer, Ridley, and others.

The Established Church of England — the fruit of the Reformation—had a form of godliness, but was minus the power.

Mr. Wesley, in 1739, organized "The United So-

cieties" for the promotion of scriptural holiness,
with only one condition previously required of those
who requested admission into them—a "desire to
flee from the wrath to come, and to be saved from
their sins." Mr. Wesley did not organize the Societies with the intention of founding a new Church,
nor did he sever his connection with the Church of
England.

"Methodist" was the name originally given to
the Wesley brothers, about the year 1729, and to
several other young men of a serious turn of mind—
members of Oxford University—who used to assem-
ble together one particular night of the week, chiefly
for religious conversation. The term was selected
in allusion to the exact and *methodical* manner in
which they performed their various engagements,
which a sense of Christian duty induced them to
undertake—such as meeting together to study the
Scriptures, visiting the poor, and the prisoners in
Oxford jail, at *regular* intervals. Subsequently it
was applied to the followers of Mr. Wesley and his
coadjutors, though he wished "the very name might
never be mentioned more, but be buried in eternal
oblivion." It was not a theoretical and premedi-
tated system, but extempore. Mr. Wesley's Rules
for the Societies say: "In the latter end of the year
1739 eight or ten persons came to me in London,
who appeared to be deeply convinced of sin, and

earnestly groaning for redemption. They desired (as did two or three more the next day) that I should spend some time with them in prayer, and to flee from the wrath to come, which they saw continually hanging over their heads. That we might have more time for this great work, I appointed a day when they might all come together, which from thenceforward they did every week—viz., on Thursday, in the evening." This he called "the first Methodist Society." Its number rapidly increased.

In 1766 emigrants came over from England or Ireland, and established themselves into a Society in New York. The recognition of the United States as an independent country, and the difference of feeling and interest that necessarily sprung up between the congregations in England and America, rendered the formation of an independent Society inevitable. The Rev. Thomas Coke, D.C.L., of Oxford University, was ordained Bishop of the infant Church, September 2, 1784. He was recognized by the Conference held at Boston, December 25 of that year. Only ninety-five years have swelled the number greatly—yes, no doubt, far beyond the most sanguine expectations of Mr. Wesley himself.

Those holding to the doctrine, as taught by Mr. Wesley, number to-day more than five million five hundred thousand. There are nearly five million children, who are not counted in the above number, cared for by, and dedicated to, God in the several branches of Methodism.

Our progress, compared with that of the most flourishing denominations of our day, has been great—yes, over two hundred per cent. greater than the most prosperous—while from our altars have gone thousands, and strengthened the ranks of our sister denominations. As the missionary spirit is now abroad in the land, and the Church seems to be waking up on the subject, there is a flattering prospect of her desire being accomplished —*"to spread scriptural holiness over the world."*

CHAPTER II.

ECONOMY.

NOTHING has added more to the progress of Methodism, perhaps, than its systematic economy. The master-mind of Wesley, guided by Divine inspiration, reëstablished the apostolic plan of itinerancy. Christ gave, first, a limited commission, to the house of Israel, but it was to go from house to house, and from town to city; it was itinerant. The second or grand commission, in Matt. xxviii. 19, was to "all nations." *"Go ye"*— it was not *stay.* The promise was to be with them "unto the end of the world."

The Prophet Elijah was an itinerant preacher. Paul never stayed more than three years at a place, and the most of his life he was on a circuit. Besides being the prophetic and apostolic plan, it is the best, for several reasons. More people can be preached to by the circuit-rider, for less cost to the Church, than in any conceivable manner. Christ knew it would be the most successful way

It is an acknowledged fact that no man can please everybody; and there is some truth in the old adage, "A new broom sweeps clean."   As some were for Paul, and others for Apollos, in olden times, so will men always be of different opinions. One man will grow stale to one congregation.   Send him to a new place, where some one else has become stale—make the exchange—and both congregations will be often benefited, and the man better situated to do good.

By the itinerant system the poor sections of country are supplied with the gospel.   Our economy sends the presiding elders, who are generally strong and good, able preachers, to every circuit and mission in our Connection, and we always try to occupy all the territory in our bounds.   We often see Churches without a pastor, whose economy is local; we seldom, if ever, see them so with us.

The disciples left *all*, and followed Jesus.   He had no conditions in his call to the ministry.   "The world is my parish" should be the motto of all who feel it to be their duty to preach the gospel.   They should be willing to be guided, or directed, by those who ask guidance of the great Head of the Church.

Congregations sometimes insist on the privilege of choosing their own pastors.   I hear of but one plausible reason for it, and that is *satisfaction*. There has been more dissatisfaction in congregational Churches, or Churches that choose their own pastors, than among the Methodists.   It is much

portant embassy. He has left the world, and appointed us in his stead, or place. An embassador is a person sent from one sovereign to another, supposed to represent in person the sovereign by whom he is sent. He must have authority. So we, as embassadors from Christ to the world, represent him, and "beseech," or "as though God did beseech you, by us, we pray you, in Christ's stead, be ye reconciled to God." In Rom. x. 15 Paul asks, "How shall they preach, except they be sent?" Dr. Clarke says: "None can effectually preach unless he has a divine mission. The matter must come from God, and the person who proclaims it must have both *authority* and *unction* from on high." A man thus called of God to preach should give his entire time and attention to his work. (This refers to pastors; the local preachers, who are not supported by the Church, have to prepare for their pecuniary wants.) When a man thus gives all his time, talent, and energies to his people, they should support him.

The support of the ministry has been "spoken against" by an ignorant set of men, until they have made some people believe that it is wrong to pay a *circuit*-rider. Intellectual men never dispute it; Bible-readers cannot but know it is right. In 1 Cor. ix. 7 Paul asks, "Who goeth a warfare any time at his own charges?" and then goes to the law to prove his position (verse 9): "Thou shalt

2

not muzzle the mouth of the ox that treadeth out the corn"—showing that it had always been God's plan for his ministers to be supported. In the 11th verse he asks, "If we have sown unto you spiritual things, is it a great thing if we shall reap of your carnal things?" If the minister feeds you on the bread of life, that will enable you to so live here as to gain a home in heaven, what is it, compared to this, if you help to supply his temporal wants while he is preaching? Besides, it being such a small thing in comparison, "Even so hath the Lord ordained that they which preach the gospel should live of the gospel." It is the will of the Lord that you should support your preacher. It is a means of grace. "God loveth a cheerful giver." Surely it is a privilege to be loved by the Lord. You will feel better, and enjoy more religion. There is a fine sentiment in

> God loveth a cheerful giver,
> 　Though the gift be poor and small:
> What doth he think of his children
> 　When they never give at all?

It is unnecessary to dwell on this part of the subject, for you are aware that it is right. The ability to pay is often called in question. You can pay your taxes. Why? Because you are compelled to do it, and make your arrangements accordingly. You should pay as much, and as willingly, for the privileges of your souls as for those of your bodies. One great mistake is, that people put off paying their preachers until all else is paid, and then frequently they have nothing to pay with, and the poor preacher is in want. If we would resolve, the first money we get, to pay our gospel-debt—for it is a debt, not charity—and when we get it, lay it away as not ours, but the preacher's, and no more spend it than if it were never ours, and when we see the steward pay it to him, or pay it to the preacher —he will always report it to the Quarterly Conference—there would be no difficulty on our part.

In order that the preacher be interesting, and have a variety to preach, he must buy books and take papers, to keep up with the times—and all of these cost money. If he should spend all his time in secular employment, as you do, he would be no wiser than you; and how could he benefit you by his preaching? By supporting your preacher you enable him to give all his time to his work, and to accomplish the more good; and you will be instrumental in this way in doing much good, not only to others, but to your own souls.

Our economy is the best the world has ever known.

CHAPTER III.

DOCTRINE—GOD.

THAT there is one God, all who read this will admit. Although we cannot comprehend thoroughly his nature, yet it is our duty to endeavor to gain a knowledge of his divine character. "God is a Spirit." From all eternity has this Spirit existed. Ps. xc. 2: "Before the mountains were brought forth, or ever thou hadst formed the earth and the world, even *from everlasting* to everlasting, thou art God." All matter—all things we can see—had a beginning, and will have an end; but God is eternal.

Omniscience is one of the attributes or perfections of God, and is plainly taught in Heb. iv. 13: "Neither is there any creature that is not manifest in his sight; but *all* things are naked and open unto the eyes of him with whom we have to do." Acts xv. 18: "Known unto God are all his works from the beginning of the world." Again, we hear David say, Ps. cxlvii. 5, "His understanding is *infinite.*" As infinite is boundless, so is the knowledge of God. It is not bounded by time or space. Throughout his dominion—earth, heaven, and hell—the illimitable bounds of immensity of space and duration are all known unto him. Small and great, animate and inanimate, material and immaterial, things past and future, are just as clearly seen and as fully comprehended as events of the present. All "power belongeth unto God" (Ps. lxii. 11), as well as *omnipresence*, or the presence of God at all places, as is taught in Ps. cxxxix. 7–10: "Whither shall I go from thy Spirit? or whither shall I flee from thy presence? If I ascend up into heaven, thou art there: if I make my bed in hell, behold, thou art there. If I take the wings of the morning, and dwell in the uttermost parts of the sea; even there shall thy hand lead me, and thy right-hand shall hold me." Prov. xv. 3: "The eyes of the Lord are in every place, beholding the evil and the good." In this *immutable* Being we find *truth*, holiness, and goodness.

"The mercy of God is the outgoings of his goodness and love in manifestations of pity and compassion for such as are in distress or affliction, or are exposed to misery or ruin. Goodness and Love look down upon the fallen race, and desire their happiness; Wisdom devises the remedy; Pity lets fall her tear of sympathy, and Mercy comes to the rescue. But while the guilty turn with indifference or scorn from all the offers of grace tendered by the hand of Mercy, Long-suffering waits with enduring patience, reiterates the pleadings of Mercy, crying, 'Why will ye die?' until Goodness, and Love, and Pity, and Mercy, and Long-suffering—having all made their appeals only to be set at naught and rejected—join with Justice and Holiness, and every perfection of God, in pronouncing upon the incorrigible their fearful and irrevocable doom."

refers to Christ. He is denominated " The true God " in 1 John v. 20. In Isa. ix. 6 he is termed " The mighty God."

All the attributes that are applied to God are also applied to Christ. It is not strange that Nicodemus said, " How can these things be ? " We are not called upon to believe the *how*, but the fact.

HOLY SPIRIT—ITS PERSONALITY AND DIVINITY.—Some vainly contend that the Spirit is the written word, or New Testament. The Spirit is not merely an *attribute*, energy, or *operation* of the Divine Being, but a personality.

The masculine pronouns are used in speaking of the Holy Spirit. John xiv. 26: " But the Comforter, which is the Holy Ghost, whom the Father will send in my name, *he* shall teach you all things." The personal pronoun *he*, the masculine gender, would not be used if a real person was not referred to. In John xvi. 7, 8, you will see the Spirit is called *him* and *he*. Again, in verses 13, 15: " Howbeit when *he*, the Spirit of truth, is come, *he* will guide you into all truth; for he shall not speak of *himself*," etc. In these two verses the personal pronoun is used ten different times. We could multiply passages if we thought it necessary.

The Spirit is represented as teaching, reproving, guiding, speaking, hearing, taking, showing, glorifying and receiving glory—all personal acts.

The *real* divinity of the Spirit could be proven by the *honors, works, attributes,* and titles ascribed to him in the Scriptures. He is represented in Matt. xii. 31 as capable of being sinned against. Job xxxiii. 4 says, "The Spirit of God hath *made* me." All the attributes of God are applied to the Spirit.

The titles applied to the Holy Ghost, or Spirit, establish his divinity perhaps more concisely and conclusively. He is called God. In Acts v. 3 Peter asked, "Ananias, why hath Satan filled thy heart" (or why have you let him fill your heart) "to lie to the Holy Ghost?" Then he says, in verse 4, "Thou hast not lied unto men, but unto God." This passage alone is sufficient to establish the Supreme Godhead of the Holy Spirit. "God is a Spirit," and the Spirit is God.

That there is only one God is admitted. We have proven from the Bible that Christ and the Holy Spirit are God. Now it is only necessary to prove that these three are one, and we will establish that. 1 John v. 7: "For there are *three* that bear record in heaven—the *Father,* the *Word* (Jesus Christ), and the *Holy Ghost;* and these *three are one.*"

CHAPTER VI.

FREE WILL, OR THE FREE MORAL AGENCY OF MAN.

THERE is a consciousness within the breast of man that enables him to know that he can act, or not act, just as he wishes. My own feelings teach me that I can write, or I can quit, just as I wish. If I can choose to act as I please in temporal affairs, I can also in eternal affairs. If I can close my mouth and not speak when I am tempted of Satan to blaspheme God's name, or if I can choose to curse, if I can blaspheme, I can also pray if I wish. There is no civilized nation of the world but regards man a free agent. Crime is punished for the reason that man is regarded as being able to avoid crime.

The Scriptures address man as a free agent. God created man

Just and right,
Sufficient to have stood, though free to fall.

"In the day that thou eatest thereof thou shalt surely die," shows that God regarded man a free moral agent. If Adam was not capable of obeying or disobeying, as he did, it could not have been just in God to punish him. In Deut. xxx. 19, God addresses man as being capable of *choosing* life: "I call heaven and earth to record this day against you, that I have set before you life and death, blessing and cursing: therefore *choose* life, that both thou and thy seed may live." Also in Josh. xxiv. 15: "Choose you this day whom ye will serve." Choosing is *determining* or fixing the will, and man is here called on to do this himself; and if he could not choose, this would be nonsense.

Christ, in Matt. xxiii. 37, says, "How often would I have gathered thy children together, even as a hen gathereth her chickens under her wings, and ye *would not!*"—showing they could, if they would. Again, John v. 40: "And ye *will not* come to me, that ye might have life." These passages plainly show that they had the ability to come, but *would not.*

John i. 29: "Behold the Lamb of God, which taketh away the sin of the world." John iii. 16, 17: "For God so loved the world, that he gave his only-begotten Son, that *whosoever believeth* in him should not perish, but have everlasting life. For God sent not his Son into the world to condemn the world, but that the world through him *might* be saved." John iv. 42: "This is indeed the Christ, the Saviour of the world." These passages are enough, though we could produce many more, to show that Christ

died for the world, and promised eternal life to
such of the world as would believe, showing that
every man's salvation depends on his own will, or
choice. Because God knows a thing, it does not
necessitate it; if so, God's knowledge would necessitate or force him to do all he does.

We will notice some of the Scripture that some
think sets forth the idea of necessity:

"Jacob have I loved, and Esau have I hated,"
cannot mean God hated Esau as man hates, nor
could it imply that God was not willing for him to
be saved; but rather a prophecy fortelling the fate
of the two nations. "Therefore hath he mercy on
whom he will have mercy, and whom he will he
hardeneth" (Rom. ix. 18). This simply means that
he has "mercy on whom he will"—that is, all—for
he says, "I will the death of none, but rather they
would all turn and live." "And whom he will he
hardeneth"—he does not will to harden any. Paul
was only trying to convince the Romans that it was
not unrighteous in God to grant eternal life unto
the Gentiles. This is all he meant. The "elect"
are those who repent of their sins and come to God
through Christ with an humble, obedient faith.

We only have space to cite a few of the passages
of Scripture that prove the universality of the atonement. John vi. 51: "And the bread that I will give
is my flesh, which I will give for the life of the

world." Our Saviour could have meant nothing but that he was "the Saviour of the *world.*" If it does not prove that all may have eternal life, it is meaningless. Again, Heb. ii. 9: "That he by the grace of God should taste death for *every man.*" Can language be more plain? Surely a person must be very incredulous who can read the language of Jesus and doubt for a moment that "God is no respecter of persons." 1 John ii. 2: "And he is the propitiation for our sins; and not for ours only, but also for the sins of the *whole world.*" 1 Tim. iv. 10: "Who is the Saviour of *all* men, specially of those that believe." An unprejudiced mind can but see that these passages prove the universality of the plan of salvation.

If there were no other—but there are many— passages proving Arminianism, the grand commission should settle it forever—Matt. xxviii. 19, 20: "Go ye therefore, and teach all nations, baptizing them in the name of the Father, and of the Son, and of the Holy Ghost: teaching them to observe all things whatsoever I have commanded you; and, lo, I am with you alway, even unto the end of the world." Mark xvi. 15: "Go ye *into all the world,* and preach the gospel to *every creature.*" Why preach the gospel to *all nations,* if *all nations* cannot be saved? Why to *every creature,* if *every creature* cannot be saved?

3

here state that repentance means a sorrow for, and
a turning away from, and a praying for the forgiveness of, sin. Matt. xxi. 32: "For John came unto
you in the way of righteousness, and ye believed
him not; but the publicans and the harlots believed him; and ye, when ye had seen it, repented
not afterward, that ye might believe him." This
passage shows that we must repent before we can
exercise saving faith. Christ says, in Luke xiii. 5,
"But except ye repent, ye shall all likewise perish"
—showing we must repent, but never saying that
repentance will justify us; but it must precede our
justification.

How can we believe we can receive pardon without asking for it? We are told to "ask, and ye
shall receive." If we ask for pardon, we shall receive it, through faith in Jesus Christ. Prayer is
one of the conditions by which faith is given. By
prayer our faith is strengthened so that we can believe, and thus believing, we are justified, or pardoned; for we read in Acts x. 43 that "whosoever
believeth in him shall receive remission of sins."
It is true, "faith comes by hearing," and as we have
heard that "whosoever calleth on the name of the
Lord shall be saved," this drives us to the conclusion that prayer is the condition we *have heard* by
which this faith comes that purifies the heart. The
idea is this: we know that "every one that asketh

receiveth," and we ask in faith, and that faith purifies the heart. As Christ and his disciples could not cast out some "devils only by fasting and prayer," as this was necessary for their faith, so is prayer necessary for our pardon, or faith that justifies. The altar of prayer, as a place of convenience, songs of Zion, prayers of the good—all are instrumental in strengthening our faith, and assisting us in laying hold of eternal life. All of these cannot justify us, or give peace and pardon, without our faith.

Faith is the only condition that will reach all cases of humanity. If justification, or purification of heart, or pardon, could be bought, the rich could get it; if by works, those who could work, and those only, could be saved. We will not here notice all the scriptures that speak of justification by faith only, for our space will forbid. We will first notice the condition of pardon in the Old Testament.

It must be remembered that we are here speaking of how a sinner is justified, or pardoned of his past sins—not how a Christian is justified. If we fail to make the discrimination, we shall find an apparent contradiction in Paul and James.

We invite your attention to Rom. iv. 3, 4, 5, 9: "For what saith the Scripture? Abraham *believed* God, and it was counted unto him for righteous-

its meaning. After much long and hard study, and earnest prayer, we have come to the conclusion that we shall here give.

The apostles were told to begin at Jerusalem, or to preach first to the Jews—a people that had always worshiped God, but were mistaken as to the manner in which Christ should come. They did not believe Jesus to be the Christ; but when the preaching of Peter, "with the Holy Ghost sent down from heaven," made them *believe*, they were "born of God." They asked, "What shall we do?" to be saved? No, but to receive the Holy Ghost. They had long been worshiping God, but had made a grievous blunder in rejecting Christ. Acts ii. 38: "Peter said unto them, Repent, and be baptized every one of you in the name of Jesus Christ for the remission of sins, and ye *shall receive the gift of the Holy Ghost.*" It seems, from the answer that Peter gave, that they wished to receive the gift of the Holy Ghost. The point of controversy is as to the meaning of "for the remission of sins." *Εις αφεσιν αμαρτιον*, in reference to the remission of sins. "For" means *in reference to*, or, in this instance, *because of*, and not *in order to;* and we have the language of Peter himself to sustain us in our belief—Acts xv. 8, 9: "And God, which knoweth the hearts, bare them witness, giving them the Holy Ghost, even as he did unto us; and put no difference between us and them, purifying their hearts by faith." Peter was here speaking of the Gentiles who had been converted, and compared their conversion with his, or that of the Jews on the day of Pentecost. Let us examine it closely. "God, who knoweth their hearts" — that is, the Gentiles' hearts—"bare them" (the Gentiles) "witness, giving them" (the Gentiles) "the Holy Ghost, as he did unto us" (Jews) at the beginning—the day of Pentecost—"and putting no difference between us" (Jews, or disciples, if you prefer) "and them" (Gentiles), *"purifying their hearts by faith;"* and as he "put no difference between" the Jews and Gentiles, and the Gentiles were told if they would *"believe"* they should receive the "remission of sins," and they had the Spirit, or Holy Ghost, to "bear them witness" that their "hearts were purified by faith," there can be no other conclusion than that the hearts of the people, on the day of Pentecost, were "purified by faith." When one's heart is purified, he is justified—pardoned—his sins are forgiven, or remitted; for the same apostle that told them that through faith they should receive "remission of sins" said their "hearts were purified by faith." *"For,"* then, in this case, must mean *because.* We will illustrate it, in order that none may be mistaken, by a note of hand. I have purchased from my neighbor, Mr. Smith, goods to the

spake these words, the Holy Ghost fell on all them which heard the word," as a witness that their hearts had been purified by faith. As these were Gentiles, so are we, and that which applied to them will apply to us. Peter did not require any thing of them but faith. He was preaching to a sinner who had repented of his sins, and prayed for the forgiveness of them; and he only required faith. He did not say (as many now vainly talk), "To him give all the prophets witness, that through his name whosoever believes," repents, confesses, and is immersed, "shall be saved," or "receive remission of sins." If these things had been necessary for the forgiveness of their past sins, he would have told them so; for it was the first sermon that had been preached to the Gentiles. We learn that "God is no respecter of persons." Peter says, "God put no difference between us" (Jews) "and them" (Gentiles), "purifying their hearts by faith," or justifying them all by faith only.

When Peter preached at Samaria, where Jesus had formerly preached to the woman at the well, salvation through faith, there was nothing in the way of obedience required; but when they "believed Philip preaching the things concerning the kingdom of God, and the name of Jesus Christ, they were baptized" (Acts viii. 12), for they were fit subjects. They had been born again, and we learn that "whosoever believeth that Jesus is the Christ is born of God." Philip only required the eunuch to "*believe with all the heart*," before baptism. He *believed* that "Jesus Christ is the Son of God," and believing this, he was "born of God," and was a fit subject for baptism.

The conversion of Paul may be cited. Acts ix. 17: "And Ananias went his way, and entered into the house; and putting his hands on him, said, Brother Saul, the Lord, even Jesus, that appeared unto thee in the way as thou camest, has sent me, that thou mightest receive thy sight, and be filled with the Holy Ghost." Saul believed what Ananias had said; for in verse 12 it is said that he had "seen in a vision a man named Ananias coming in, and putting his hands on him, that he might receive his sight;" and of course when it came to pass, he *believed* it. His faith justified him; for he says in Rom. v. 1: "Therefore being justified by faith, *we* have peace with God through our Lord Jesus Christ." He was told to "arise and be baptized" —not to pardon his sins, or justify him. "Wash away thy sins" was to be done by "calling on the name of the Lord," prayer being necessary to produce the faith that purifies the heart.

Paul at Antioch, after preaching to the people of the genealogy of Jesus, and his life, death, burial, and resurrection, then tells them that "through this

man is preached unto you the forgiveness of sins,"
and in the next verse (Acts xiii. 39) he tells both
what forgiveness is, and how it is obtained: "And
by him *all that believe* are justified from *all things*,
from which ye could not be justified by the law of
Moses."

We will refer to only one more case—that of the
jailer, or "keeper of the prison." It is unnecessary to give this history, as all are familiar with it.
Acts xvi. 30: "And brought them out, and said,
Sirs, what must I do to be saved?"—the only time
this question is asked in the Bible. The answer is
so simple that I cannot see how men can be mistaken in its meaning. Verse 31: "And they said,
*Believe on the Lord Jesus Christ, and thou shalt be
saved*, and thy house." This needs but little com-
ment. The jailer was a sinner. When he saw the
miracle he was convinced of sin, or convicted. He
was sorry for his sins—was repenting of them—
praying for their forgiveness, or to be saved—for
"prayer is the soul's sincere desire," and it was his
desire to be saved. When he asked the men what
he "must do to be saved," they answered him as *we*
answer men who now ask the same question—"*Believe* on the Lord Jesus Christ, and thou *shalt be
saved*."

Ask those who now claim to know what you
"must do to be saved," and one will say, "Wait

until the Lord's good time," and another will cry, "Obey!" What is meant by "obey?" "Believe, repent, confess, and be immersed."

One says that if these things are not expressed, they are implied. Suppose I should tell my neighbor that he could have my bridle for five dollars. When he comes after it, he claims the saddle and horse. I would say, "I sold you only the bridle." "O," he replies, "the saddle and horse were understood!" What would you think of such a man? You would think, at least, that he had a vivid imagination. And what would you think of a man who, knowing that the New Testament says that all who believe on the Lord Jesus Christ shall be saved, should say, "O immersion is understood!" We think he could imagine more than has ever been expressed. When a man has a bridle, of course it is supposed he has a horse. So when a man is *justified by faith*, he should be obedient.

We shall next refer to some of the passages in the Epistles. Rom. iii. 26, 28, 30: "To declare, I say, at this time his righteousness; that he might be *just*, and the *justifier* of him which believeth in Jesus." "Therefore we conclude that a man is *justified by faith* without the deeds of the law." "Seeing it is one God, which shall justify the circumcision *by faith*, and uncircumcision *through faith*." Rom. v. 1, 2: "Therefore being *justified*

by faith, we have peace with God through our Lord
Jesus Christ; by whom also we have access by faith
into this grace wherein we stand, and rejoice in
hope of the glory of God." Rom. iii. 21, 22, 25:
"But now the righteousness of God without the law
is manifested, being witnessed by the law and the
prophets; even the righteousness of God, which is
by faith in Jesus Christ unto all and upon all them
that believe." "Whom God has set forth to be a
propitiation *through faith in* his blood to declare
his righteousness for the remission of sins that are
past, through the forbearance of God." Rom. iv.
5: "But to him that worketh not, but believeth on
him that justifieth the ungodly, his faith is counted
for righteousness." Gal. iii. 26: "For ye are all
the children of God *by* faith in Christ Jesus." 1
John v. 1: "Whosoever believeth that Jesus is the
Christ is born of God." Gal. iii. 22–24: "But the
Scripture hath concluded all under sin, that the
promise by faith of Jesus Christ might be given to
them that *believe.* But before faith came, we were
kept under the law, shut up unto the faith which
should afterward be revealed. Wherefore the law
was our schoolmaster to bring us unto Christ, that
we might be *justified by faith."* These quotations
might be greatly multiplied; but the foregoing are
surely satisfactory to such as are disposed to abide
by the plain declarations of Scripture.

We will now prove by the following scriptures that justification is not of works. Rom. iii. 20, 27, 28: "Therefore by the *deeds of the law* there shall *no* flesh be justified in his sight; for by the law is the knowledge of sin." "Where is boasting, then? It is excluded. By what law? of *works?* Nay, but by the law of *faith.* Therefore we conclude that a man is *justified by faith without the deeds of the law.*" Obedience can but be by works. Rom. iv. 4, 5: "Now to him that worketh is the reward not reckoned of grace, but of debt. But to him that *worketh not,* but *believeth* on him that justifieth the ungodly, his faith is counted to him for righteousness." Gal. iii. 2, 11: "This only would I learn of you, Received ye the Spirit by the *works* of the *law,* or by the hearing of *faith?*" "But that no man is justified by the law in the sight of God, it is evident; for, The just shall live by faith." Gal. ii. 16: "Knowing that a man is *not* justified by the *works* of the law, but by the faith of Jesus Christ, even we have believed in Jesus Christ, that we might be *justified by the faith* of Christ, and *not* by the *works* of the *law;* for by the *works* of the *law shall no* flesh be justified." This is sufficient to establish the truth that we are not justified by *works.*

St. James, in speaking of how a *Christian* may be justified, or *remain* just after he has been justi-

4

which is derived from βάπτω (*bapto*), and means to baptize. Webster defines baptism as "the application of water to the body as a religious ceremony." This may be done either by sprinkling or pouring—simply *affusion.* A person when immersed may be baptized, for as he is pushed under or through the water, it rushes up, or is caused to rush up, and thus may be *applied* to his body. Immersion *can* be scriptural; baptism *is* scriptural.

We will show in every instance that *baptism was* practical, and in many cases that *immersion was not.*

The first baptism on record is referred to in 1 Cor. x. 2, "And were all baptized unto Moses in the cloud and in the sea." In the first verse Paul says, "I would not that ye should be ignorant, how that all our fathers were *under* the cloud, and" how they "were baptized." We find, notwithstanding Paul's desire, that many at the present day are very ignorant of the *modus operandi* of their baptism. We will let the Bible tell us.

---

ent relations: (1) Water baptism, Matt. iii. 11; (2) John's baptism, Matt. xxi. 25; (3) Holy Ghost baptism, John i. 33; (4) Fire baptism, Acts ii. 3; (5) In the name of the Lord Jesus, Acts xix. 5; (6) Baptism for the dead, 1 Cor. xx. 29; (7) Baptism of suffering, Luke xii. 50; (8) For remission of sins, Acts ii. 36; (9) Baptism of the Spirit, 1 Cor. xii. 13; (10) Baptized into Christ, Rom. vi. 3; (11) Buried with Christ in baptism, Rom. vi. 4; Col. ii. 12.

Read from Ex. xiii. 20 to the close of chapter fourteen. Notice the 21st verse of the thirteenth chapter, "And the *Lord* went before them by day in a pillar of a cloud, to lead them the way." Verse 19, chapter fourteen, says, "And the angel of God, which went before the camp of Israel"— the "Lord" is here termed the angel of God—"removed and went behind them; and the pillar of the *cloud went from before* their face, and stood behind them." This "*cloud went* from before them, and stood behind them;" before they were between the "walls" that were "on their right-hand and on their left." Then they could not have been immersed by being surrounded by water and cloud. *How* then were they baptized? We are told in Ps. lxxvii. 17, "The *clouds poured* out water," and baptized them. Read from the 15th verse, and you will find that David had reference to this event. They were there in the sea, near the water's edge, and were baptized by the cloud *pouring* out water upon them as it passed over from before them behind them.

We will next consider "John's baptism." We wish to state in the outset that the most learned Baptist of our age, and all Protestants or Pedobaptists, agree that John's baptism was not Christian baptism.

The first mention of John's baptism is in Matt.

iii. 6, "And were baptized of him in Jordan." The
preposition *in*, that only denotes the *place where* he
baptized, bothers some, and causes them to think
he immersed. He could baptize *in* Jordan as
well as immerse. I have baptized people *in* creeks
by pouring. How? They would kneel down
near, or in, the water, and I would pour the water
on them, as John did. In the 11th verse he tells
how he baptized. Says he, "I indeed baptize you
with water." If I should tell you that I whipped
a man *with* a stick, you would understand me. You
would know I applied the stick to the man, not the
man to the stick. *In Alexandria* tells *where*, and
with a stick tells *how;* so "in Jordan" tells where,
and "with water" tells how. "He shall baptize
you with the Holy Ghost and with fire." This
came to pass on the day of Pentecost. Acts ii. 2:
"And suddenly there came a *sound* from heaven as
of a rushing mighty wind, and it"—the sound, parse
for yourself—"filled all the house where they were
sitting." Verse 3: "And there appeared unto them
cloven tongues like as of fire, and it sat upon each
of them." What "sat upon" them? The "cloven
tongues of fire." Verse 4: "And they were all filled
with the Holy Ghost." "All" the people—not the
house. Now read verses 16 and 17: "But this is
that which was spoken by the Prophet Joel: And
it shall come to pass in the last days, saith God, I

will *pour* out of my Spirit upon all flesh." We find, then, that when they were baptized by the Holy Ghost and with fire, it was done by "pouring out" of the Holy Ghost. We find that John did his baptizing by pouring.

Says one, "Jesus was baptized *in* Jordan, and 'coming up straightway *òut of* the water.'" How is that, if he was not immersed? I will tell you: He was in the water one or forty inches, as the case might have been, and John "baptized him with water," as he did all others, by applying the water to him.

"In Enon, near to Salim, because there was much water there," is not mysterious; for "much water" was necessary for the immense crowds that came to his baptism. Enon was only an inn or tavern, and the "much water" is several springs. Why do not immersionists refer to "where John first baptized?" They are as shy of it as "Nostrum" (my horse) is of a tanyard. John x. 40: "And went away again beyond Jordan into the place where John at first baptized, and there he abode." The next two verses plainly teach us it was some nice *dry* place. He says, "And many resorted unto him, and many believed on him *there.*" He could not have immersed, for a place where the people would "resort," where Jesus "abode," and where they could stay long enough for "many to believe on him there,"

was not a place to immerse.   But he could baptize
there very well.   This is enough of John's baptism.
One who would not believe this surely "would not
be persuaded though one should rise from the dead."
    We will now consider the personal baptisms.
    Acts viii. 38 : "And they went down both into the
water, both Philip and the eunuch, and he baptized
him."   Because "they went down into the water"
is no reason the eunuch was immersed; for "baptized" does not mean to *dip*, but the "application
of water to the body," not the body to the water.
There are several things to take into consideration
in this case.   "From Jerusalem to Gaza, which is
desert," there is but little if any running water to
baptize in.   The eunuch was reading just after
where Isaiah (for the book was not then divided
into chapters as it now is) had said, "And he shall
sprinkle many nations."   How did Jesus "sprinkle
many nations?"   The Bible is its own interpreter,
and makes it plain.   We read, " When Jesus made
and baptized more disciples (though Jesus baptized
not, but his disciples)."   And his command to his
disciples was, "Go ye, therefore, and baptize [or
sprinkle] all nations."   And when Philip explained
it to him thus, it is the most reasonable conclusion
that "when they went down into the water" the
eunuch desired that Philip should baptize him *with*
the water.

Paul (Acts ix. 18) was baptized in a *city*, Damascus, in the house. Immersion is unreasonable in this case. I will relate a similar case: I went to Nashville, into a street called College, in the house of Smith, and found Saul of Tarsus, when I went in, laid my hands on him, "scales fell from his eyes," or he "*professed* religion," and arose immediately, and was baptized. No place here for immersion, if baptize meant to immerse.

Cornelius and his children next.

Acts x. 47, 48: We only know that Peter asked, "Can any man forbid water, that these should not be baptized, which have received the Holy Ghost as well as we? And he commanded them to be baptized in the name of the Lord." There are only two things directly from which we can derive the desired information: 1. "Can any man forbid water" to be brought? is the only intelligent interpretation or explanation that can be given. Let water be brought, and these be baptized, here in the house; as we have never heard of any one in the apostle's time journeying to any water to baptize. 2. The meaning of the word *baptize* settles it forever.

We will here invite your attention to the jailer and his children. Of course, he and his children were all baptized alike.

Acts xvi. 33: "And he took them the same hour of the night, and washed their stripes; and was baptized, he and all his, straightway." **There** are several things in this instance I desire you to notice: 1. It was death by the Roman law for a jailer to leave his post. If he had done so he would have been put to death, which he was not; therefore, he did not leave and seek a stream to be immersed. 2. There is no proof or probability that there was any bath in the prison; therefore, there is no probability of immersion. They had water, to be sure, in washing their stripes—if he washed them with water—and a small amount of that could have been used. This is the only reasonable conclusion.

"But," says the immersionist, "they went out of the jail, and could they not have found water sufficient in which to immerse?" Hold! do n't be too sure they went out of the prison until you consider the matter well. We see, in verse 23, "they cast them *into prison,*" charging the jailer to keep them safely. Verse 24: "Who, having received such a charge, thrust them *into* the *inner* prison." They are now in twice. They are "into prison" and "into the inner prison," or cell. They must come out of two doors before they can be where they were before their incarceration. In verse 30 it says, "And brought them out" of the *inner* prison, or cell, of course. They are still in the prison, but not the *inner* prison. That prison was like all other prisons: the jailer's family-room and the "inner prison," or the cells, were all under the same inclosure. The jailer had no authority to take them out of prison. "They"—the magistrates—"cast them into prison;" but the jailer "thrust them into the *inner* prison." The jailer "took them out" of the "inner prison." And the next morning, or "when it was day, the magistrates sent the sergeants, saying, Let those men go." "But Paul said unto them, They have beaten us openly uncondemned, being Romans, and have cast us into prison, and now do they thrust us out privily? nay, verily; but let them come themselves and fetch us out." This shows they never left the prison. The jailer and all his family were baptized—water applied to the body—in jail, or prison.

Why contend for immersion when the word is not in the Bible? Being buried with Christ in, or by, baptism, has no reference whatever to the mode of baptism, but shows that we are buried or "hid with Christ in God." Affusion is the Bible mode of baptism.

INFANT BAPTISM.—We will first prove by history that infants have long been the subjects of baptism. We will just refer you to "Chambers's Encyclopedia," Vol. II.: "When the Jews proselyte from another Church, they require the males—both grown and babies—to be circumcised; all must bring a sacrifice, and all—both the adults and the babies—had to be baptized." Chambers, who "wrote for the million," has too much at stake to be the least biased to any denominational credulity. This corresponds with the figure used in Isa. xl. 11. In speaking of the coming of Christ, he says: "He shall feed his flock like a shepherd; he shall gather the *lambs* with his arms, and carry them in his bosom." We learn from ancient history that the Eastern shepherds wore a blanket over their shoulders, with a belt around their waist; when they found lambs so young and weak that they could not travel, they would put them in their bosoms—made by the belt and blanket—and carry them home and feed them with warm milk. We find this prophecy came to pass in the life of Christ, for "Jesus took them"—children, or lambs—"up in his arms and blessed them." We should consider him a poor shepherd that would shelter the old sheep and leave out the tender lambs. Not only did the Jews practice infant baptism before and after the coming of Christ, but we will now prove by reliable ancient history that the apostles preached it. Origen, who wrote one hundred and eighty-five years after the birth of Christ, says, "The Church received from the apostles an order to give baptism to infants" (Ruter's Gregory, p. 40). I insist on your seeing the authors, and then think if there is any thing but blind prejudice and ignorance that will cause any to publicly affirm that infant baptism is a child of the dark ages.

Again, we would refer you to Justin's Apol., I. p. 57, who wrote forty years after John. He says, "Many persons among us, sixty or seventy years old, were made disciples"—baptized—"of Christ in their infancy, continue uninterrupted. Children of the good are deemed worthy of baptism."

We wish to cite you to history of different centuries, to show that infant baptism has been practiced by the Church in all ages.

"Fidus, two hundred and fifty-four years after the birth of Christ, applied to Cyprian, Bishop of Carthage, to know whether the baptism of infants ought to take place the eighth day after their birth. Sixty-six bishops said it was not necessary to defer it to the eighth day, and that baptism should be given to all, especially to infants."—*Cyprian's Ep.* 59, 66.

Again, Augustin, who wrote in the fourth century, said: "Infant baptism, which the whole Church practice, was ever in use. The whole Church has ever held to it. I have never read or heard of any Christian, whether Catholic or Sectary, that held otherwise." Pelagius says the same. There were some individuals, prior to this time, that wished to defer the baptism of infants until just before their death, because they thought baptism washed away their sins; but if in danger of dying, they were strong advocates of it.

Tertullian, in the beginning of the third century, was the *first* to oppose infant baptism in any form, and he did it because he thought baptism washed away all past sins, and that sins committed after baptism were peculiarly dangerous. He desired, therefore, that baptism should be postponed until just before death.

Peter de Bruis, in France, A.D. 1200, was the next to oppose it. His reason was because he thought infants incapable of salvation.

The first to oppose it because they *thought* it unscriptural were German Baptists, in the beginning of the sixteenth century.

In the face of these facts, some men have ex· posed their ignorance of history by saying that infant baptism began in the fourth century, without giving us any proof of their assertion. We have proven by reliable historians that it was practiced by the apostles and all the primitive Christians—with a few exceptions—up to the seventeenth century.

We will now show that infant baptism is scriptural. All will admit that infants were embraced under the Abrahamic covenant. (Gen. xvii. 10–14). Then we have only to show that the covenant made with Abraham is the same as the Church under the gospel dispensation, more fully unfolded. The gospel is a new dispensation of religion, but not a new Church. The Church underwent many changes. It is only necessary to give a few quotations to prove that the covenant of Abraham was the Church. Acts vii. 38: "This is he that was in the Church in the wilderness," etc. Ps. xxii. 22: "In the midst of the congregation [Church—*kahal* —ἐκκλησία] will I praise thee." Heb. iv. 2: "Unto *us* was the *gospel preached* as well as unto *them.*" 1 Cor. x. 4: "And did all eat the same spiritual meat, and did all drink the same spiritual drink; for they drank of that spiritual Rock that followed them, and *that Rock* was Christ." John xiii. 36: "Abraham rejoiced to see *my* day, and saw it, and was glad." There can be nothing more direct than Matt. xxi. 43: "Therefore I say unto you, The kingdom of God shall be taken from you (Jews), and given to a nation bringing forth the fruits thereof." Not a *new* kingdom made or set up, but the same kingdom, or Church, taken from the Jews and given to the Gentiles. Therefore, the Jewish and the Christian Church are the same. Paul, in comparing the Church to an olive-tree, perhaps borrowed it from Jer. xi. 16: "The Lord called thy name, A green olive-tree, fair, and of goodly fruit; with the noise of a great tumult he hath kindled fire upon it, and the branches of it are

broken." St. Paul, in speaking of the rejection of
the Jews on account of their unbelief, and the ad-
mittance of the Gentiles into the Church, does not
say that the olive-tree was destroyed, and another
tree planted. Hear him in Rom. xi. 15–24: "For
if the casting away of them be the reconciling of
the world, what shall the receiving of them be, but
life from the dead? for if the first-fruit be holy, the
lump is also holy; and if the root be holy, so are the
branches. And if some of the branches be *broken
off*, and thou, being a wild olive-tree, wert graffed
in among them, and with them partakest of the
root and fatness of the olive-tree, boast not against
the branches. But if thou boast, thou bearest not
the root, but the root thee. Thou wilt say, then,
The branches were broken off, that I might be
graffed in. Well; because of unbelief they were
broken off, and thou standest by faith. Be not high-
minded, but fear; for if God spared not the natural
branches, take heed lest he also spare not thee.
    And they also, if they abide not still in un-
belief, shall be graffed in; for God is able to graff
them in again. For if thou wert cut out of the
olive-tree, which is wild by nature, and wert graffed
contrary to nature into a good olive-tree, how much
more shall these, which be the natural branches, be
graffed into their own olive-tree?"
    Dr. Ralston says on this subject that "the scope

of the apostle's reasoning is so plain here that it cannot be misunderstood by an intelligent, unbiased person. The Jews were originally embraced in Church-relation with Abraham and the heads of the Jewish Church, who are represented as the first-fruit,' which was 'holy'—that is, they were consecrated, or set apart in a sacred Church-relation, presented under the emblem of a 'good olive-tree.' For they were 'broken-off' branches of unbelief.' In this same tree, or covenant relation and Church-privileges, the believing Gentiles were ingrafted. But did the rejection of the unbelieving Jews destroy the primitive Church of God into which they had been taken? By no means. The unfruitful branches 'were broken off,' but the original stock remained. The 'good olive-tree' yet ' stood firm, and into the same stock the Gentiles were ingrafted. Now we demand, unless the New Testament Church is a continuation of the original Church established in the family of Abraham, is *essentially* the same, though under a change of dispensation, how is it possible to place any sensible construction on the language of St. Paul in the passage presented? We confidently affirm that the passage admits of no other interpretation; and, if so, does it not follow that as infants were by divine appointment received into the Abrahamic Church, therefore they still retain the right of Church-mem-

5

bership derived from the original charter, and consequently they have a right to baptism? The only possible way to escape this conclusion will be to show that the law of God conferring upon infants, in the days of Abraham, the right to covenant and Church-privileges has been repealed under the gospel; but this never has been, and, as we are sure, never *can* be done."

Baptism came in the room of circumcision. They are signs and seals of the same covenant. Circumcision was the initiatory rite into the Church in the days of Abraham and of Moses; so baptism was the initiatory rite into the Church in the days of Paul and Peter. Circumcision was the token of visible membership in the Church of God, and covenant of old; so is baptism now. Circumcision pointed to the remission of sins by the atonement of Christ, to regeneration and sanctification of the spirit; so does baptism. Circumcision has passed away, and baptism occupies the same relation to the Christian Church as circumcision did to the Jewish. The children were circumcised and brought into the Church under the Old Dispensation, and they always have been and always should be baptized and brought into the Church under the New.

We wish to call attention to a few of the prophecies of the Old Testament in reference to the Gentiles and their children.

Isa. xlix. 22: "I will lift up my hand to the Gentiles, and set up my standard to the people; and they shall bring thy sons in their arms, and thy daughters shall be carried upon their shoulders." There is no other sensible conclusion only that "thy sons and daughters" here mean the children, and "shall bring" them to the Church. And as baptism is the initiatory rite into the Church, they were baptized into, or initiated by baptism into, the Church.

Isa. lii. 15: "So shall he sprinkle many nations," or baptize them by sprinkling water upon them. This came to pass in the commission, "Go ye, therefore, and baptize all nations." We have referred to the passage stating that "Jesus himself baptized not, but his disciples." He sprinkled, or baptized, all nations through his disciples. Infants are a part of "all nations," therefore he baptized infants.

As we will now notice the New Testament on this subject, we will farther consider Christ's language in Matt. xxviii. 19: "Go ye, therefore, and teach all nations, baptizing them in the name of the Father, and of the Son, and of the Holy Ghost." "Teach" here means proselyte, or make disciples of. First, we would do well to consider that this language was spoken to the Jews, who were always accustomed to see the children of all that they "taught," or that were proselyted from other Churches, baptized, as we proved in the beginning of this subject. They were commanded to baptize "all nations." Children compose a large part of all nations, therefore they were commanded to baptize children. They were first commanded to proselyte them—for this is the meaning of μαθητεύσατε —and after they are proselyted then baptize them, and then teach as they are competent to be taught.

We wish to refer you next to the Saviour's language in reference to infants. Luke ix. 48: "Whosoever shall receive this child in my name receiveth me." (Mark x. 13–16; Luke xviii. 15–17.) By reading all the passages cited, you will see they were small "infants," for "Jesus took them up in his arms." There is only one way that I have ever heard of to receive children in the name of Jesus, and that is by baptism. In what way could a Baptist receive a child in the name of Jesus?

The "kingdom of God," here used, means the Church on earth, for all children are not members of the Church in heaven, for they may live to years of maturity, die in their sins, and be lost. If I should say, with a child on my knee, that of such is our school, all would understand that the school is *composed* partly, at least, of such; so with the Church—it means that the Church is composed partly of children.

Paul says, in 1 Cor. x. 1, 2, "*All* our fathers were under the cloud, and all passed through the sea, and were *all* baptized unto Moses in the cloud and in the sea." No one can deny that there were *small infants* baptized here.

We will next notice very briefly the actions of the apostles after they received the commission to "baptize all nations."

Peter, on the day of Pentecost (Acts ii. 39), says, "The promise is unto you, and to your children." If he did not wish to convey the idea that children were to be baptized, he used the wrong language; for the Jews were accustomed to seeing the children of proselytes baptized, and Peter had, in the preceding verse, commanded them to be baptized.

The apostles baptized several households. Acts xvi. 14, 15: "And a certain woman named Lydia, a seller of purple, of the city of Thyatira, which worshiped God, heard us; whose heart the Lord opened that *she* attended unto the things which were spoken of Paul. And when she was baptized, and her household, *she* besought us, saying, If ye have judged me to be faithful to the Lord, come into my house, and abide there." All the particulars specified are of "Lydia," and nothing is said of the piety or conversion of her "household," only they were "baptized." *She* "worshiped God."

She "heard us." "The Lord opened *her* heart."
She "attended unto the things spoken." *She* said,
"If ye have judged *me* to be faithful, come into
my house." The only explicable reason for so much
being said about *her*, and nothing being said of
her *household*, is, her household were *children* who
were baptized on the faith of their parents.

Again (Acts xvi. 30–35), when the jailer asked,
"What must I do to be saved?" the answer was,
"Believe on the Lord Jesus Christ, and thou shalt
be saved, and thy *house.*" The jailer "was baptized, *he* and *all* his (children) straightway." The
word was preached to "all that were *in* his house,"
but does not say they were baptized. "And *he* took
them, and (*he*) washed their stripes." "*He* brought
them into *his* house ; *he* set meat before them." *He*
"rejoiced," and *he* was "believing in God *with* (or
in company with) all his house." If there had
been adults, surely some would have helped him in
some of the work. No one believed or rejoiced in
God but him ; yet they were all baptized.

If there were no infants baptized in all the household baptisms, the apostle's language is calculated
to lead astray both Jews and Gentiles. There are
other household baptisms, and many other passages
we might quote to establish this truth, but enough
has been said to be conclusive to the unprejudiced
mind. We will sum it all up in this :

1. Infant baptism was practiced by the Jews before and during the days of Christ. Neither Jesus nor the apostles ever condemned it; therefore, they thought it right.

2. Children were members of the Church under the Old Dispensation. The law was never repealed, nor objected to, by Jesus or his apostles.

3. Profane history tells us it was practiced by the apostles and primitive Church.

4. The Bible condemns evil of all kinds, and especially the pernicious customs of the Jews; it does not condemn infant baptism, but both in the Old and New Testaments it is set forth in unmistakable terms; therefore, for these four reasons, we believe infant baptism is right.

CHAPTER IX.

ADOPTION.

WHEN we are converted it is our privilege to know it. This knowledge is communicated by the Spirit of God to our hearts. Only a few passages are necessary to prove this point, as it is very generally admitted. The Spirit is the witness to give us this evidence of our adoption.

Peter, in Acts xx. 8, says: "God, which knoweth the hearts, *bare them witness*"—how? By "giving them the Holy Ghost," or Spirit, which is the same. That we may have the direct witness of the Spirit, or Holy Ghost, in our hearts to let us know we are children of God, will be seen from the following scriptures. Rom. viii. 15, 16: "For ye have not received the spirit of bondage again to fear; but ye have received the Spirit of adoption, whereby we cry, Abba, Father. The Spirit itself beareth witness with our spirit, that we are the children of God." 1 John v. 10: "He that believeth on the Son of God *hath the witness in himself.*" 1 John iii. 14: "We *know* that we have passed from death unto life, because we love the brethren"—we have a consciousness of our acceptance with God. Mr. Wesley speaks of it thus: "The testimony of the Spirit is an inward impression on the soul, whereby the Spirit of God directly witnesses to my spirit that I am a child of God, that Jesus Christ has loved me, and given himself for me, and that all my sins are blotted out, and that I, even I, am reconciled to God."

WRITTEN CREED, OR DISCIPLINE.—"Let your moderation be known to all men." There is a class of bigots, generally very ignorant, who wish to make people believe that they are the only people in the world who are governed by the Bible. They cry, "The Bible! the Bible! We have no creed but the Bible!"—as if no one else ever read or believed the Bible. There is one thing clearly demonstrated—they have a creed, mental, verbal, or written, if they have any *sense*. An opinion is a creed. There is no more harm in having a written creed than a mental or verbal one. If one has an opinion in his mind, and does not express it, it is a mental creed; if he speaks it, it is an oral creed; if he writes it, it is a written one.

There are so many *silly* objections to creeds, professions of faith, and disciplines, that I will not try to notice them all, but show the propriety of a *written* creed.

Written creeds prevent confusion. I remember

once reading a long editorial in a religious, or denominational, journal, in which the editor tried his
best to establish the fact that we ("Christians") had
a right to pray for the conversion of sinners. He
had no creed but the Bible, he claimed. He believed it, and why not publish his belief in a short
form, so that the world could know what he thought
on that subject? But in a few days one of his brethren, and a cousin, I think, came to the village to
preach a series of sermons to the people who had
read the journal above referred to. In one of his
sermons he tried for nearly two hours to prove that
we did *not* have any right to pray for the conversion
of sinners. Whom must the people believe—the editor, or his cousin? Neither of them had any creed
but the Bible. They claimed to have no Procrus-
tean bedstead to be shortened or stretched to until
they fitted it. No, thought I, the preacher was not
letting the Bible be his iron bedstead. A written
creed would let us know where they stand; but as
it is, if you say they teach that we have no right to
pray for sinners, one will cry, " We are persecuted! "
and if you say they teach that we have a right to
pray for sinners, then another cries, " Persecution! "

Without some understanding, opinion, or creed,
we could have no uniformity in worship. One who
reads the Bible thinks public worship should con-
sist of song, prayer, sermon, and the sacrament.

Another thinks that songs are of human institution, and should be avoided; and another thinks that prayers should not be offered in public. One thinks the sacrament should be taken every Lord's-day, just after the *morning* service; another contends that we should follow our Lord's example, and take it at night. One thinks singing should be done standing; another, sitting. These are all guided by the Bible.

Creeds and Disciplines prevent misunderstandings. How often do we hear the cry, "Persecution! persecution! We are persecuted! we are misrepresented!" Write your opinions, and we will not misrepresent you. You can do this, and no sensible person will say you are governed by your Discipline. You can do it without adding to or taking from the Bible. There is no more adding to the Bible by writing your belief in a Discipline than there is in writing a religious paper or a good book. We repeat, all who read the Bible, and have sense enough to think, have their *belief* in reference to the fundamental doctrines and duties of Christianity, whether *mental, spoken,* or *written.*

We once worshiped in the same house with two distinguished no-creed divines. My intercourse with them resulted in the following conversation:

"Brethren, do you believe the Bible?"

"Yes," they both very kindly responded.

" You are governed by the Bible alone—have no written creed ? "

" Most assuredly," they said.

" Please tell me what you believe."

"*I* believe the Bible ! "   "*I* believe the Bible ! " they eagerly exclaimed.

"I am young; will you be so kind as to give me some information? "

" With the greatest of pleasure," they said.

" Well,* is Jesus Christ God ? "

" Yes," said B., "God was manifest in the flesh."

" No," said C., "' This is my beloved Son.' "

' "Is man totally depraved ? "

B. " Yes ; 'Man is as prone to evil as the sparks to fly upward.'"

C. " No ; but he is only disposed to sin."

" Has the sinner the right to pray ? "

B. " Yes.   Paul says, 'I would that men pray everywhere.'"

C. " No ; 'for we know that God heareth not sinners.' "

B. " But that is the language of an unregenerate man."

" Hold ! hold !   I do not wish to spring a discussion ; but how is a man justified, or pardoned ? "

B. " By faith only."

---

* Pay attention, now, and I will give you their creed, *written* as they spoke it.

C. "By obedience, faith, repentance, confession, and *baptism.*"

"How is a man baptized?"

B. and C., in one voice. "By immersion."

"What is baptism *for?*"

B. "A door into the Church."

C. "For the remission of sins."

"*Who* should be baptized?"

B. "Those who can give an experience of grace."

C. "Penitent believers."

"Who should take the sacrament?"

B. "Only those who have been immersed by a regular minister of *our* Church, and have never annulled their baptism by leaving *our* Church."

C. "All the followers of Christ."

"Who is a proper administrator?"

B. and C. "O well"—and here was confusion.

"Can a Christian apostatize?"

B. "No. 'He that doeth these things shall never fall.'"

C. "Yes; a man baptized *into* Christ may die and be lost—go to hell—in Christ."

"When was the kingdom set up?"

B. "In the days of John the Baptist."

C. "On the day of Pentecost."

"What is the best form of Church-government?"

They both seemed glad the church-bell rung for

church, and the conversation closed without an answer to the last question.

Now, take the questions and their answers sepa-
rately, and you will have both of their creeds *written.* They believed and preached what they said
to me ; and why not write it, so that the world may
know what you believe?

I will give some reasons why they will not write
their faith : (1) They change it as often as a Ban-
tam-rooster crows from day-break to sunrise, or as
often as they see fit. (2) There is no agreement
among themselves. (3) If written, they could not
so well preach and practice one thing here, and
somewhere else deny it, as I have known them to
do. (4) If written, the world would know it, and
would never indorse it. (5) Their errors would be
exposed.

CHAPTER X.

SANCTIFICATION.

PERFECTION, sanctification, and holiness, are synonymous. In an age of so much formality as the present, and of struggling for riches, ease, and comfort, it is not strange that some deny, and others doubt, that Christian perfection is attainable in this life. Nor would it be very surprising to me if some should believe, at no distant day, that it is impossible for us to remain justified in this life, as those professing justification live so far beneath their duty. Therefore, because so few are perfect, is no reason that it is not attainable in this life. We are aware of the fact that some paint sanctification in too glowing colors, while others obscure it with clouds and mist.

In order to understand this glorious theme, we will first notice what is *not* meant by perfection. (1) It does not imply *absolute* perfection, as God is perfect; (2) nor *angelic* pefection—we are not perfect, as angels are; (3) nor are we perfect, as Adam was; (4) we are not perfect in *knowledge*—we can never "know as we are known" of God in this

life; (5) we shall never be so perfect in this life
as to be free from *mistakes;* (6) nor infirmities.
Viewing it, then, in this light, it will not be so
offensive.

Sanctification *is* higher attainment in religion,
that enables the Christian to fully develop the prin-
ciples and practices of Christianity—entire sanctification, Christian perfection, perfect holiness, perfect love, and the maturity of all the Christian
graces—to be free from sin, to live without sin.

We will now prove by the Scripture that sanctification is attainable in this life. We are not to
prove that *you* are free from sin: we are only to
prove that it is possible for man to live without sin.
As sanctification, perfection, and holiness, are synonymous, we shall so consider them.

Gen. xvii. 1: "Walk before me, and be thou
perfect." If Abraham could not have lived perfect, God never would have made the demand; he
does not require impossibilities. Matt. v. 48: "Be
ye therefore *perfect,* even as your Father which is
in heaven is perfect." As God is perfect in his
sphere, so "be ye perfect." Deut. x. 12: "And
now, Israel, what doth the Lord thy God require
of thee, but to fear, and to love, and to
serve the Lord thy God with *all thy heart,* and with
all thy soul." Serve God with a *perfect heart* and a
willing mind. Ezek. xxxvi. 25: "Then will I

sprinkle clean water upon you, and ye shall be *clean;* from *all* your filthiness, and from *all* your idols will I cleanse you." Job i. 1 : "There was a man in the land of Uz, whose name was Job, and *that man* was *perfect.*" No one can doubt that perfection was attainable in Job's day. Why not yet ? It is, as has been testified by thousands living and dead.

As perfection is strongly set forth in the Old Testament, we shall see it more so in the New Testament. Hear the language of Jesus (John xiv. 23): "If a man love me, he will keep my words; and my Father will love him, and we will come unto him, and make our *abode* with him." Do you think Jesus and his Father will abide where sin is? Again (John xvii. 23): "I in them, and thou in me, that they may be made *perfect* in one." Zacharias said (Luke i. 74, 75), " Being delivered out of the hands of our enemies, might serve him without fear, in holiness and righteousness before him, *all* the days of our life." Matt. xxii. 37 : "Thou shalt love the Lord thy God with *all thy heart,* and with *all thy soul,* and with *all thy mind.*" The language of the apostles is too plain to be misunderstood. Rom. xiii. 8 : "He that loveth another hath *fulfilled* the law." 1 Tim. i. 5 : "Now the end of the commandment is charity out of a *pure heart.*" 1 John i. 9 : "If we confess our sins, he is faithful

6

and just to forgive us our sins, and to cleanse us from *all unrighteousness.*" 1 John iv. 12: "God *dwelleth* in us, and his love is *perfected* in us." "Cleansed from *all their filthiness,* and from *all* their *idols,* and *all* their unrighteousness," and "to serve him in *holiness* and *righteousness all the days* of our life, and to serve him with a *perfect heart,*" can imply nothing less than Christian perfection, holiness, or entire sanctification. We will only cite one more passage—1 Thess. v. 23, 24: "And the very God of peace *sanctify you wholly;* and I pray God your *whole* spirit, and *soul,* and *body* be preserved *blameless* unto the coming of our Lord Jesus Christ. Faithful is he that calleth you, who also *will do it.*" Do what? Answer his prayers by *sanctifying them wholly.*

We could give many more as strong as those above; but they are sufficient for an honest inquirer after truth. (For a fuller argument on this subject see Smith's and Ralston's "Elements of Divinity," Wesley's and Marvin's sermons on Christian Perfection, Entire Sanctification, and Going on to Perfection.)

Is sanctification attainable in this life? Yes; for God commanded us to "be perfect" (Gen. xvii. 1). God never requires an impossibility. Luke xv. 7: "Be ye holy." If it were not possible to be holy, God would never have commanded it.

Perfect love is possible only to the sanctified. Luke x. 27 : "Thou shalt love the Lord thy God with *all thy heart.*" We cannot obey this commandment only in this life. It is attainable in this life; for we are commanded to "follow peace with all men, and *holiness,* without which *no man shall* see the Lord" (Heb. xii. 14), after death, in peace.

All the Scripture we have cited, to prove that "perfected holiness in the sight of God " is possible at all, proves that it is possible in this life; for "there is no work, nor device, nor knowledge, nor wisdom, in the grave whither thou goest."

"But," says some poor, doubting soul, "does not John say, 'If we say we have no sin, we deceive ourselves, and the truth is not in us;' and, 'If we say we have not sinned, we make him a liar?'" We have never thought of saying that we never did sin. John was there only telling them they *had* sinned; for " all have sinned and come short of the glory of God," in time past. Read 1 John i. 7–10, and we will see that the apostle was only impressing us with the idea that we have committed sins in time past, that we should fully realize the existence of natural corruption, that we must confess our sins, and that He is "faithful and just to forgive us our sins, and to cleanse us from *all unright-eousness.*"

How sanctification may be obtained shall next

have our attention. This, like conversion, may be either instantaneous or gradual. There is only one condition of sanctification—that is faith in Jesus Christ. There are several things necessary to this blessing, while faith is the condition of it.

We must realize the fact of inbred sin, or natural corruption; that no sin is excused with God, for God cannot look upon sin with the least degree of allowance. Still we must have *holiness*, without which "no man shall see the Lord." *Entire* consecration is necessary—we must consecrate ourselves *wholly* unto God. "Do all to the glory of God." When thus consecrated to God, ask him 'to *sanctify you wholly;*" and "as your faith is, so be it unto you." If you are doubtful—cannot believe—say, in the language of the father, "Lord, I believe; help thou mine unbelief;" and thus believing, you can realize that "the blood of Jesus Christ cleanseth from *all* sin." Then we can "rejoice evermore." O may all who read these pages have that holy peace, love, and comfort!

CHAPTER XI.

THE SACRAMENTS.

ST. PAUL wrote "as the Spirit gave him utter-
ance." The Spirit, seeing the future as well as
the present, and knowing the contentions that would
arise, and the diversity of opinions that would occur
in reference to the sacrament of the Lord's Supper,
moved St. Paul to pen language that should forever
settle this question (1 Cor. xi. 28, 29, 31): "But let
a man examine himself, and so *let* him eat of that
bread, and drink of that cup. For he that eateth
and drinketh unworthily, eateth and drinketh damnation to *himself,* not discerning the Lord's body."
"For if we would judge *ourselves, we should not be
judged.*"

Notwithstanding these plain declarations of the
Scripture, directly upon this subject, we hear men
judging who are worthy. They never ask men to
examine *themselves;* but *they* examine them, contrary to the Bible, and then "let them eat," if they
measure up to their standard. Brother, stop and
think. Are you not violating the plain teachings
of the Bible?

There is only one condition required of any one who desires to take the Lord's Supper, and that is *conversion to God.* Those who partake of the sacrament commune with Christ, the *Head* of the body; and if they can commune with the Head, they have a right to commune with the entire body, or whole Church. The only conclusion at which we can arrive is that "*close* communion" is unscriptural.

Says an objector, "It is close baptism." Nonsense! The Bible says nothing about baptism being necessary to communion. The communion did not originate in denomination, sect, or party. Neither Luther, Knox, nor Wesley originated it; it is neither a Baptist, Presbyterian, Campbellite, nor Methodist table; it is the Lord's table, and all the Lord's people are invited to it. We shall show that it is not close baptism. If I should be immersed into your Church to-day, to-morrow leave it, and join the Christian Baptists, who practice free communion—there being none of your faith near—next Sunday you would not permit me to commune. I have not annulled my baptism, for I was not rebaptized. You see, it is not *close baptism.*

"But," continues the close communionist, "we are the only Church, and you are not in the *Church,* and therefore you are not entitled to commune with it." We deny it all; and we have the question until you prove yours, which you never have done, and never can do. You have surely forgotten what Paul says—"Let a man examine *himself*," while you are examining him; and, "if we would judge *ourselves*, we *should not be judged;*" and you are judging us, and it is contrary to the Bible. It does not say, Let Paul examine Peter, and Peter others, but let every one—Peter, Paul, James, and the Church—examine *themselves*—not you examine me, as you are doing.

Christian baptism cannot be a prerequisite to communion, for the Supper was first instituted. It was instituted before the death of Jesus, and Christian baptism afterward, in his commission to his apostles (Matt. xxviii. 18–20). John's baptism was not Christian baptism; for he did not baptize in the name of Christ, and his disciples were rebaptized when they embraced the gospel (Acts xix. 1–5).

"Should there not be a rule, or standard, by which we may know who ought to commune?" says the objector. The apostles admitted all "believers" to the privileges of the Church; and Paul said, "*Let a man examine himself.*" The objector says: "We have no authority to expel from other Churches unworthy members, and one of our expelled members might go and join some other

Church, and commune with us." That would not
injure you. If he "eateth and drinketh unworthily," he "eateth and drinketh damnation to himself," not to you. Besides, other Churches are as
careful as yours. There are as many "tares" in
"the wheat" in your fields as in ours. Jesus, the
spotless Lamb of God, ate, or communed, with
Judas after the devil had entered into him.

There is only one other objection that we will
notice, and that is *offense.* Many close commun-
ionists are convinced that it is right to commune
with all good people; but their Church forbids it,
and therefore they will not do so, for fear they
may be turned out of the Church. There might
be some prudence in considering whether we should
withdraw from such a Church, or not; but as to
whether "we ought to obey God rather than man,"
is the question for us to settle. Is it right? If so
—and surely you cannot deny it—should you vio-
late your own conscientious views to please the
erroneous views of an erring Church? Can you
afford to do *wrong,* and please a few of your own
small Church, rather than do *right,* and please a
majority of the Christian world and your Saviour?
Would you not rather do *right,* and please Jesus,
even if it should displease some poor, erring mor-
tal, than do *wrong,* and please your friends, and
displease Jesus?

The day is dawning when there will be a grand revolution in this direction. When such men as Hall and Spurgeon raise the banner of Free Communion, superstition, ignorance, and bigotry can no longer "hold the fort," but will give up to the milder and better theme of brotherly love.

CHAPTER XII.

THE UNCONDITIONAL FINAL PERSEVERANCE OF THE SAINTS.

CAN Christians so apostatize, or fall away, as to be lost? Not that there is a desire to fall, but *can* they?

As we think our position is understood, we shall now proceed to show that they *can*.

1. Angels from heaven fell. Jude 6; "The angels which kept not their first estate" fell; and "if God spared not the angels that sinned, but cast them down into hell," neither will he spare us; therefore we, being less holy, and exposed to temptation, may fall.

2. Adam fell. None will say they are purer than he. He was pure, had never been contaminated with sin, was not morally corrupt, as we are, had no depraved nature, as we have—yet, amid all his purity, he yielded to temptation, and fell. We, being less pure, may fall.

3. Our third argument is based upon the fact that others have fallen. David, "a man after God's own heart," fell. He was guilty of murder

and adultery; for he had Uriah killed in order that he might have Bathsheba, his wife; and it "displeased the Lord" (2 Sam. xi.). Solomon, the favored of the Lord, was guilty of adultery and idolatry. Judas "by transgression *fell.*" Jesus never would have given him the power to work miracles had he not been a good man. The "devil entered into him" on the night of the betrayal. Peter denied his Lord. Peter had no "spark," for he cursed and swore, and lied willfully and knowingly. Ananias and Sapphira "lied unto the Holy Ghost, and unto God." Hymeneus and Alexander "have made shipwreck" (1 Tim. i. 19, 20). These cases are too plain to be misunderstood. If persons, under both the Old and New Dispensations, have fallen, persons under the New, or now, may fall.

4. Conscience dictates to us that we can fall. You know that you can cease praying and going to church. You feel that you can give way to your fleshly and carnal desires. You are conscious that you *can* let your passions run at large. You *feel* and *know* that you *could* jest, dance, drink to excess, gamble, lie, steal, and blaspheme the name of God. If you do these things, you have not a doubt that you will fall away. But to the law and the testimony.

5. Our argument, in the fifth place, will be to

prove from the Old Testament that a Christian—one that is holy—may so "fall from grace" as to be eternally lost. Thus saith the Lord by the prophet (Ezek. xviii. 24): "When the righteous turneth away from his righteousness, and committeth iniquity,　in his trespass that he hath trespassed, and in his sin that he hath sinned, shall he die." This cannot mean *self*-righteousness, for it says, "when he turneth away from his righteousness and committeth iniquity;" and it cannot mean temporal death, for it says, "in his sin that he hath sinned shall he die;" and no one dying in his sins can be saved. In Ezek. xxxiii. 13 it is unmistakably plain: "When I shall say to the righteous, that he shall surely live; if he *trust in his own righteousness, and commit iniquity*, all his righteousness shall not be remembered; but for his iniquity that he hath committed, he shall die for it." While "God hath loved us with an everlasting love," and has said, "My covenant *I* will not break, and I will not fail David," yet it is clear that we can wander from God, and that his love will give place to his justice. *He* will not break *his* covenant, but *we can* and *may* break it, and fail to love him. We could multiply passages from the Old Testament, showing how many had fallen, and the warnings given to Israel not to fall, but these are sufficient.

6. We will now notice a few of the very many

passages in the New Testament, bearing directly on this subject. Jesus, looking down through the coming years, saw the danger of apostasy, and said (John viii. 51), "If a man *keep* my saying, he shall never see death." "If" shows there is a probability and danger of him not keeping it, and if he fails, he shall "see death" unless he repents. In John x. 27, 28, Jesus says: "My sheep hear my voice, and I know them, and they follow me; and I give unto them eternal life; and they shall never perish, neither shall any pluck them out of my hand." There is no unconditional salvation there; for he says, "*My* sheep;" and after they have wandered off, and are devoured by the wolf, they are no longer his sheep, nor can they longer "hear his voice." They are not "following" him; and the eternal life is suspended on the condition that they follow him. And "they shall never perish" if they "follow me;" "neither shall any man pluck them out of my hand;" but they can get out if they wish. "If ye do these things, ye shall never fall." Fail to do them—fail to "hear" and "follow"—and you will fall. We find that final salvation is on the condition of our "doing these things." Jesus represents himself as a "vine," and his followers as the "branches," or limbs, and tells by this illustration what will become of them if they "abide not" in him, or if they prove unfaithful.

John xv. 1–6: "I am the true vine, and my Father is the husbandman. Every branch in me that beareth not fruit he taketh away. I am the vine, ye are the branches. If a man abide not in me, he is *cast forth* as a branch, and is *withered;* and men gather them, and cast them into the fire, and they are burned." It would be difficult for one to form language stronger than this. These are persons represented as being in Christ; but they are taken away from Christ by the Father, because they bear no fruit. They are beyond recovery; they are burned—no chance to graft them in, and cause them to bear fruit. The plain meaning of this parable is, if we fail to be good and bring forth fruit as Christians, we shall lose our religion. It can mean nothing less.

7 We shall next consider what the Apostle Paul says on this subject. Rom. xi. 17–22: "And if some of the branches be broken off, and thou, being a wild olive-tree, wert graffed in among them, and with them partakest of the root and fatness of the olive-tree, boast not thyself against the branches; but if thou boast, thou bearest not the root, but the root thee. Thou wilt say, then, The branches were broken off, that I might be graffed in. Well; because of unbelief they were broken off, and thou standest by faith. Be not high-minded, but *fear.*" What for? "For if God spared not the natural

branches, take heed lest he also spare not thee. Behold therefore the goodness and severity of God : on them which *fell,* severity ; but toward thee, goodness, *if thou continue* in his goodness ; otherwise [if not] thou also shalt be cut off." He, no doubt, was addressing Christians. There was danger of their being cut off—not only from the Church militant (for a sin, unrepented of, that would exclude him from the Church would also exclude him from heaven)—but from the favor and friendship of God. "God is faithful, who will not suffer you to be tempted above that ye are able" (1 Cor. x. 13) ; but if you fail to obey when it is said, "Quench not the Spirit ; 　*hold* fast that which is good ; 　abstain from all appearance of evil"—that "your whole spirit, and soul, and body be preserved blameless unto the coming of our Lord Jesus Christ ; faithful is he that calleth you, who also will do it "— if you fail to fear, and watch, and pray, and be not high-minded — fail to fulfill all these conditions — you cannot obtain these promises. *" Otherwise thou shalt be cut off."* There is no contradiction between this and Rom. viii. 38, 39 : " I am persuaded that neither death, nor life, nor angels, nor principalities, nor powers, nor things present, nor things to come, nor height, nor depth, nor any other creature, shall be able to separate us from the love of God, which is in Christ Jesus our Lord." This is all

true—angels, wicked men, and all the combined
powers of earth and hell, cannot separate us; but
we can separate ourselves. "My grace is sufficient
for thee," if you will use it; use grace, and grace
will be given. Paul, although confident that these
could not move or separate him if he did his duty
and trusted in God, yet feared, lest a promise being
left us of entering into that rest, some of us should
come short of it. And 1 Cor. ix. 27: "But I keep
under my body, and bring it into subjection, lest
that by any means, when I have preached to others, I myself should be a castaway." He had just
said (verse 24), "So run, that ye may obtain." If
a believer cannot become a disbeliever—if one in
hope of eternal life cannot become hopeless—if we
cannot "so run that we may" not "obtain"—why
all this warning? Is one-third of the Bible a meaningless fable? "O it is to make us faithful!" says
one. "God is not a man, that he should lie"
(Num. xxiii. 19). He would not have said, "If
they turn away from their righteousness they shall
surely die," if he had not meant it. Paul never
would have had the impression that we could "fall
away," and be lost, if there had been no possible
chance to have done so. You cannot make me believe that Paul would have palmed a falsehood off
on the Church. If there had been no danger, he
would probably have used such language as this:

"You will be better and happier here if you do your duty; but if not, you will be saved anyhow. No use of fearing; no use of annoying yourself about falling away; no danger of being cut off." Not so—Paul knew the danger. He felt, no doubt, as we all should feel who are called to preach—"So thou, O son of man, I have set thee a watchman" upon the walls of Zion; and "if thou dost not speak to warn the wicked from his way, his blood will I require at thy hands. Therefore, thou son of man, say unto the children of thy people, The righteousness of the righteous shall not deliver him in the day of his transgression; neither shall the righteous be able to live for his righteousness in the day that he sinneth." Again (Heb. vi. 4–6): "It is impossible for those who were once enlightened, and have tasted of the heavenly gift, and were made partakers of the Holy Ghost, *if they shall fall away*, to renew them again unto repentance; seeing they crucify to themselves the Son of God afresh, and put him to an open shame." Paul tells them here what will be the consequence if they *fall away*—shows, beyond doubt, there is a possibility of a fall. We could reason on this subject at length, but we deem it unnecessary. This is so "plain, the wayfaring man, though a fool, need not err therein." The same inspired writer says again (Heb. x. 38): "The just shall live by

7

faith; but if any man draw back, my soul shall have no pleasure in him"—meaning, "drawing back to perdition; I shall utterly cast him off." Again (Heb. x. 26-29): "If we sin willfully after that we have received the knowledge of the truth, there remaineth no more sacrifice for sins, but a certain fearful looking for of judgment and fiery indignation, which shall devour the adversaries. He that despised Moses's law died without mercy under two or three witnesses. Of how much sorer punishment, suppose ye, shall he be thought worthy, who hath trodden under foot the Son of God, and hath counted the blood of the covenant, wherewith he was sanctified, an unholy thing, and hath done despite to the Spirit of grace?" The person here spoken of was *sanctified*. He knowingly and willfully sinned; therefore, "there remaineth no more sacrifice for sins"—he was lost.

8. We will notice, in this connection, what the Apostle Peter says of those that "have escaped the pollutions of the world;" if,"they are again entangled therein, and overcome," what is their condition? 2 Pet. ii. 20, 21: "*If* after they have escaped the pollutions of the world through the knowledge of the Lord and Saviour Jesus Christ, they are *again* entangled therein, and *overcome*, the latter end is worse with them than the beginning. For it had been better for them not to have known the way of

righteousness than, *after they had known it, to turn from* the holy commandment delivered unto them." Could stronger language have been written? He not only says they may be "'overcome," but that it "is *worse* with them than the beginning," or before they were converted. "But," says one, "the next verse tells us that 'the dog is turned to his own vomit again; and the *sow*, that was washed, to her wallowing in the mire.'" So it does; but the "*dog*" was a well dog, and the "*sow*" was "*washed.*" We are nothing but dogs and sows, when compared with God; but here they were *well* and *clean.*

9. We will now only quote a few passages, and leave this subject for your prayerful consideration. "Many of the Jews turned back." Isa. i. 28: "And they that forsake* the Lord shall be consumed." Jer. ii. 13: "For my people have committed two evils; they have *forsaken* me the fountain of living waters, and hewed them out cisterns, broken cisterns, that can hold no water." Matt. x. 22: "He that *endureth to the end* shall be saved." Matt. xii. 43, 45: "When the unclean spirit is gone out of a man, he walketh through dry places, seeking rest, and findeth none." "Then goeth he, and taketh with himself seven other spirits more wicked than himself, and they enter in

---

*Forsake—to leave. We cannot forsake that which we never possessed, or to which we were never attached.

and dwell there; and the *last state of that man is worse than the first.*" Heb. iv. 1: "Let us therefore fear, lest, a promise being left us of entering into his rest, any of you should seem to come short of it." Heb. ii. 2, 3: "For if the word spoken by angels was steadfast, and every transgression and disobedience received a just recompense of reward, how shall we escape if we *neglect* so great salvation?" Heb. iii. 14: "For we are made partakers of Christ, *if* we hold the beginning of our confidence steadfast unto the end." 1 Cor. x. 12: "Wherefore let him that thinketh he standeth take heed lest he *fall.*" 1 Tim. i. 19: "Holding faith, and a good conscience; which some having put away concerning faith, have made shipwreck "—lost all. Rev. ii. 4, 5, 10: "Nevertheless I have somewhat against thee, because thou hast *left* thy first love. Remember therefore from whence thou art fallen, and repent, and do the first works; or else I will come unto thee quickly, and will remove thy candlestick out of his place, except thou repent." "Be thou *faithful unto death*, and I will give thee a crown of life." We could give many other passages bearing directly on this subject, but we deem the above sufficient.

"If they do fall," says one, "they can never be renewed." Well, that is begging the question, or equivalent to saying they can fall. As you have assumed that ground, we will now prove they can.

CHAPTER XIII.

BACKSLIDERS RECLAIMED.

THAT there is an unpardonable sin we will not deny. Matt. xii. 31, 32: "All manner of sin and blasphemy shall be forgiven unto men; but the blasphemy against the Holy Ghost *shall not be forgiven unto men.*" This is attributing the works of Jesus to the devil. We believe there are many that "make shipwreck" of their faith, and become so wicked, after their conversion, that the last end is worse than the first; "for it had been better for them not to have known the way of righteousness than, after they have known it, to turn from the holy commandment delivered unto them." Yet we believe they can be renewed. After they have so fallen away as to be finally lost, if they should thus die, we think they can be saved by *returning* to Jesus by faith.

We will first clear away the brush; when all difficulties are removed, we will then proceed to give you the law and testimony.

The stronghold of those who contend that a backslider cannot be reclaimed is Heb. vi. 4–6: "For it is impossible for those who were once enlightened, and have tasted of the heavenly gift, and were made partakers of the Holy Ghost, and have tasted the good word of God, and the powers of the world to come, if they shall fall away, to renew them again unto repentance; seeing they crucify to themselves the Son of God afresh, and put him to an open shame." In order to comprehend the meaning of this passage, we must understand to whom it was addressed, etc. The Christian Hebrews were converts from Judaism. While they were Jews they did not believe Jesus to be the Christ. Now, for them "to fall away" was to renounce Christianity and go again to Judaism. In doing this they openly and publicly said that Jesus was an impostor, and died a just death on the cross, and never rose from the dead; thus "crucifying to themselves the Son of God afresh, and putting him to an open shame," by saying he was an impostor. Therefore, "there was no more sacrifice for (their) sin." Should they remain in this belief—that he was not the Christ—"it *is* impossible to renew them again unto repentance"—that is, impossible to *get* them to repent—not impossible for them *to* repent. If they should become convinced of their error, and again believe "that Jesus is the Christ," there would then be a "sacrifice for sin," and then they could be renewed unto repentance.

You see there is no difficulty in the way here when we understand what Paul means.

The next stumbling-block is Heb. x. 26–29: "For if we sin willfully after that we have received the knowledge of the truth, there remaineth no more sacrifice for sin, but a certain fearful looking for of judgment and fiery indignation, which shall devour the adversaries. He that despised Moses's law died without mercy under two or three witnesses; of how much sorer punishment, suppose ye, shall he be thought worthy, who hath trodden under foot the Son of God, and hath counted the blood of the covenant, wherewith he was sanctified, an unholy thing, and hath done despite unto the Spirit of grace?"

This we must view in a similar light as the one above. The reason "there remaineth no more sacrifice for sin," to them, is because they "have trodden under foot the Son of God," the only sacrifice for sin; and if they refuse him as the sacrifice, "there remaineth no more sacrifice for sin." Of course, if they "counted the blood of the covenant, wherewith they were sanctified, an unholy thing," there was no other "sacrifice for sin." And while they thus willfully persisted in the belief that it was an "unholy thing," there could be nothing "but a certain fearful looking for of judgment and fiery indignation, which shall devour the adversaries." But should they be convinced that the "blood of the covenant" is a "holy thing," then there is still a "sacrifice for sin," and all who wish can obtain forgiveness of sin.

As we have explained the passages that look most forbidding to the backslider, we will now cite you to the invitations of God to come. We will not use a passage where the backslider is not included. We will first notice those where the backslider alone is invited.

Isa. lv. 7: "Let him *return* unto the Lord, and he will have mercy upon him; and to our God, for he will abundantly pardon." A man can never *return* to a place where he has never been. Here the "wicked and unrighteous" backsliders are invited to come, or return. Return means to go back. Hos. vi. 1: "Come, and let us *return* unto the Lord; for he hath torn, and he will heal us; he hath smitten, and he will bind us up." These are precious promises to the poor apostate to get him to return. Hear him again in Hos. xiv. 1, 4: "O Israel, *return* unto the Lord thy God, for thou hast *fallen* by thine *iniquity*." "I will heal their *backsliding*, I will love them freely; for mine anger is turned away from him." Mal. iii. 7: "Return unto me, saith the Lord, and I will return unto you."

We could give many others of this character if we thought it necessary. These are sufficient to encourage the prodigal to return to his Father's house.

We will now invite your attention to the universal invitations, such as embrace all men.

Isa. lv. 1: "Ho, *every one* that thirsteth, come ye to the waters, and he that hath no money; come ye, buy, and eat." All who have any desire for salvation are here invited to come, "without money and without price." *All* men *desire* to be saved, therefore all men are here invited to come.

Hear the words of the blessed Jesus himself, Matt. xi. 28: "Come unto me, all ye that labor and are heavy-laden, and I will give you rest." Are you weary of your sins? Are you heavy-laden with guilt? Then you are invited to come to Jesus, and he "will give you rest." If there were no other passages in the Bible, this would be sufficient; but there are many.

The backslider can be saved, for God commands *all to repent,* and he does not command impossibilities.

Acts xvii. 30: "The times of this ignorance God winked at, but now commandeth *all men everywhere* to repent." If "all men" could not receive pardon, it would be mockery to command them to repent.

The unlimited love of God is another strong argument in favor of our position. We are told in John iii. 16, "For God so loved the *world*, that he gave his only-begotten Son, that *whosoever* believeth in him should not perish, but have everlasting life." "For God sent not his Son into the world to condemn (any of) the world, but that (all) the world through him might be saved." God gave his Son to save the world; backsliders are a part of the world, therefore they can be saved. As we quoted extensively from this class of Scripture in our argument on the extent of the atonement, we deem it unnecessary to enlarge here.

We are persuaded thus of "Religion: if you seek it, you will find it; if you find it, you will know it; if you know it, you have got it; if you get it, you can lose it; if you lose it, you can find it.'

APPENDIX.

THE law-making body of Methodism is the General
Conference. It is composed of all the bishops, and
an equal number of clerical and lay delegates from each
Annual Conference. There is one clerical delegate for
every thirty traveling preachers, and an equal number of
lay members. It meets quadrennially, or every four years,
in the month of May. It generally continues in session
from twenty to thirty days. It has the power to change
the usages, but not the power, of our Church.

The Annual Conference meets every year. It is composed of all the itinerant preachers within its bounds.

The bishop is the president of the Annual Conference.
It receives preachers on trial who wish to join the itinerant ranks. When they have traveled two years, and
passed the required examination, they are then received as
members of the Conference, and ordained deacons. After
traveling two more years, and completing the course of
study, they are then ordained elders.

It is the duty of this Conference to examine the character of all its members, and transact the business laid down
in the Discipline. Here the preachers receive their work
for the ensuing year. The bishop, aided by the presiding
elders, appoint the preachers to their fields of labor. Four

(107)

lay delegates from each presiding elder's district are also members of the Annual Conference.

The District Conference also meets once a year. It is composed of all the preachers and officers of the district. A district is composed of from ten to fourteen circuits, stations, or missions. The presiding elder is the president of the District Conference, and it is held by him—when no bishop can be had to review the work within the bounds of his district.

The Quarterly Conference is held four times a year, in each charge, by the presiding elder, or by the preacher in charge in his absence, to transact the business of the circuit, or charge. Here the stewards report, and hand over to the preachers the money collected to bear their expenses while they are preaching. The Quarterly Conference is held where the members thereof may determine by vote, but it generally meets in rotation. If there are four appointments in a circuit, each place generally has a quarterly meeting once a year.

The Church Conferences are to be held in each church at least once every three months (but, alas! how many fail!) They are held by the preacher in charge, to transact the business connected with that charge, or Society.

"There is only one condition previously required of those who desire admission into these Societies—a desire to flee from the wrath to come, and be saved from their sins."

"Seekers" may join our Church, and be baptized when, and in the manner, they wish.

The sacrament of the Lord's Supper is generally administered once a month in stations, and once every three months on circuits, and at quarterly meetings.

A deacon in our Church is not authorized to administer

the Lord's Supper. He can perform the ordinance of baptism, and solemnize the rite of matrimony. The elder alone administers the Lord's Supper.

No person can (lawfully) join our Church without publicly assuming the vows of the Church before the congregation; nor can any leave it privately. They can ask to have their names erased from the Church-book, and then it is the pastor's duty to announce it publicly.

In moving from one neighborhood to another, even if not to remain more than a year, a Church-letter should be obtained from the preacher, to prevent the loss of Church-membership; for twelve months' absence strikes off your name.

Those who feel that they are unworthy a place in the Church, and wish to leave it, should make the fact known to their pastor.

There seems to be a proneness among Church-members to partake of the amusements of the day. We earnestly beg you to take the Discipline, and prayerfully read "The General Rules." Ask yourselves if you are "doing what we know is not for the glory of God"—such as "the taking such diversions as cannot be used in the name of the Lord Jesus." Are jesting, dancing, dram-drinking, attending the gambling operations of the turf, the theater, or the circus, glorifying God? Can you use such diversions "in the name of the Lord Jesus?" No; it would be solemn mockery. When you are doing such things you are positively, willfully, and knowingly violating the rules of the Church you have vowed to support.

Now, turn to the baptismal vows, and read: "Dost thou renounce the devil and all his works, the vain pomp and glory of the world, with all covetous desires of the same, and the carnal desires of the flesh, so that thou wilt not follow or be led by them?" *Answer.* "I renounce them all." Are you not breaking your baptismal vows when you are participating in those amusements which are the glory of the world to follow? Yes, most assuredly you are. Amusements that are innocent in themselves may, and often do, become harmful in their degree or association.

"Young persons of cultivated minds and elegant manners, who may desire to be sincerely religious, are especially open to danger, from the tone of surrounding fashionable society, and from the plausibility of the worldly spirit. But the law of *gratification* which rules the world, and offers the present and immediate 'gratifications only,' is, and ever must be, opposed to the unbending law of *duty*, which conscience and God imposes. There can be no compromise here. There can be no inward experience of grace, no valid religion of the heart, which is not preceded by a full, unreserved, irrevocable commitment to the Lord. This commitment involves self-denial, taking up the cross, and following Christ. Such a religion needs not, desires not, allows not, participation in worldly pleasures, in diversions which, however sanctioned by position, are felt and known to be wrong by every truly awakened heart. Its spiritual discernment is not declined by well-dressed plausibilities, by refinement in taste, or respectabilities in social position. It has 'put on the Lord Jesus,' and made 'no provision for the flesh to fulfill the lusts thereof.' The influence of this form of religious character may be silent, but it is none the less potent, in the family, by the fireside, at the watering-place, or on the broad thoroughfares of business. What the Church *lives* alone affects the world."—*Bishops' Address.*

We wish to give one word of exhortation, in reference

to the prevailing evil of fretfulness, which weakens the power of Christianity, especially in the family. When the children see this manifestation of sin, it destroys their confidence in their parents. It also infuses a like disposition of disagreeableness to those with whom we associate.

Kindness is one of the characteristics of Christianity; and, to "manifest ourselves to every man's conscience," we must carry our religion into the parlor, family, and every-day business of life.

The world has set up a high standard for Christianity, and we must measure up to it. Let us *live* and *die* our religion. This ever has and ever should characterize Methodism.

THE END.

easier for a dozen wise, experienced men to choose a suitable pastor for a Church than it is for those who in some instances are very young and inexperienced to elect a man whom they often know but little, if any thing, about. If one should become dissatisfied with the pastor, in their Church, unless a majority of the members should also become dissatisfied, he might remain so a life-time without any remedy, while we have the assurance of a change every four years, and if there is much dissatisfaction—but there seldom is—he may be changed in one year, or at once.

Exhorters are those who are not called to preach, but feel that they have inclinations to exhort sinners publicly to repent. This should not be left for all to do of their own choice, independently; for in this way unsuitable persons might impose upon the Church. An exhorter is not a preacher. He may use a passage of Scripture as a foundation for his exhortation, but must not take a text. Persons who cannot preach, or expound the word of God, may effectually exhort sinners.

Licensed preachers have power, or permission, to preach, but not to solemnize the rite of matrimony, or to administer the sacraments of the Church. Four years as a local preacher, or two years as a traveling preacher, renders the licentiate eligible to election as deacon. The Bible says, "Lay hands suddenly on no man," to ordain him. We think this good advice. Deacons are permitted to solemnize the rite of matrimony, baptize candidates for Church-membership, and assist the elder to administer the sacrament of the Lord's Supper. One who has been a local deacon four, or a traveling deacon two, years may be ordained elder.

The elders are exhorted to feed the flock; but the bishop is to oversee the whole Church. From very early times there have been bishops to oversee the Church (1 Tim. iii. 5). Some object to bishops on the ground of their authority. The Bible gives them the authority, and bids you "obey them that have the rule over you, and submit yourselves" (Heb. xiii. 17). The ordination of the ministry in the apostolic age, by the laying on of hands, was not for any miraculous gift of the Spirit, but a Church-form, to be observed continually.

Preachers should be divinely called. We do not mean that one hears an audible voice; but as sounds falling on the ear make impressions on the mind, so our conscience is moved by the influence of the Spirit, making us *feel* that we ought to preach. One man saying that no one is called to preach because he is not, is poor sophistry. Paul says "we are embassadors for Christ," executing the function of an embassador in Christ's stead. He came from the Father to mankind on this im-

CHAPTER IV

CHRIST—HIS DIVINITY.

THE humanity of Christ is generally admitted; and his entire personal history proves him to be man, or the "Son of man." But that Jesus Christ is truly God is what we wish here to prove. Christ is called the Lord and God in Isa. xl. 3: "The voice of him that crieth in the wilderness (John the Baptist), Prepare ye the way of the Lord (Christ), and make straight in the desert a highway for our God" (Christ). And we find this passage quoted and applied to Christ in Matt. iii. 3: "For this is he that was spoken of by the Prophet Esaias (Isa. xl. 3), saying, The voice of one crying in the wilderness, Prepare ye the way of the Lord," etc. John i. 1: "In the beginning was the Word (Christ), and the Word was with God, and the *Word* (Christ) *was God.*" This is as plain and forcible as language can make it, that Jesus Christ is called God, and as none but God is called God, Jesus must be God. In Matt. i. 23 Jesus Christ is called "God with us." In Rom. ix. 5 he is called "God blessed forever." "God was manifest in the flesh." 1 Tim. iii. 16

CHAPTER V

SCRIPTURES.

FIRST. *Sufficiency for Salvation.*—We believe "the Holy Scriptures contain all things necessary to salvation," and without adding to or taking from them, we indorse them as the will of God to man. Many of the prophecies of the Old Testament are fulfilled. A great many of the types and shadows, sacrifices and offerings, are done away with. "All Scripture is given by inspiration of God, and is profitable for *doctrine*, for reproof, for correction, for instruction in righteousness: that the man of God may be perfect, thoroughly furnished unto all good works." The inspired apostle said, in Acts viii. 32, "The place of the *Scripture* which he read was *Esaias the Prophet*," showing that all the Old Bible is "profitable for doctrine." All the moral precepts are still binding on us. Salvation in the Old Testament was offered through a *prospective* Saviour; salvation in the New Testament is offered through *retrospective* faith in Christ, who has died for our redemption.

Second. For the sake of harmony, we think it

best to have our faith, or opinion, *written*, so that the world may know what we believe and teach. There can be no impropriety in it. It is not adding to nor taking from the Bible. It is only giving our opinion to others. Some seem to wish to make the impression that we are not governed by the Bible, or that we never study it; or, if we do, we are not capable of comprehending its meaning. If *we* preach what we believe the Bible to teach, they cry "Persecution! persecution!" At the same time they think that we should come and hear them preach what they believe, and think strange if they hear any complaint from us, while they often use a tirade of abuse that should be beneath the dignity of a Christian gentleman. All this we must peaceably take, and never return a word, or some one is dreadfully persecuted. This ingenious scheme of proselyting has hoodwinked and decoyed some unstable souls off where there is nothing but spiritual drought, and they have lost all of the enjoyment of their religion, if not their souls.

Third. *Original Sin—Depravity.*—"As in Adam all died" a temporal and spiritual death, and he is our federal head and representative, we are all thus dead, which is total depravity. As our opinion without the Bible is worth nothing, we will give you a "Thus saith the Lord" for all we do.

Man before the flood was "only evil." Gen. vi.

5: "And God saw that the wickedness of man was great in the earth, and that every imagination of the thoughts of his heart was only evil continually." Gen. viii. 21: "For the imagination of man's heart is evil from his youth." This "evil" is not brought about by education, example, association, or *otherwise,* but it is "from his youth." Sin is the cause—either directly or indirectly—of all trouble; and it is said in Job v. 7, "Man is born unto trouble, as the sparks fly upward." David speaks of himself in language like this in Ps. li. 5: "Behold, I was shapen in iniquity; and in sin did my mother conceive me." Not that his mother and father were sinners practically, but naturally. There could have been no moral rectitude in David. Again, Ps. lviii. 3: "The wicked are estranged from the womb: they go astray as soon as they be born, speaking lies."

The total depravity of man is very forcibly spoken of in Jer. xvii. 9: "The heart is deceitful above all things, and desperately wicked: who can know it?" "The heart" here spoken of is not the heart of the worst of men only, but the generality of men. If man were not depraved, there would be no necessity of the new birth. Jesus says, in John iii. 3, "Except a man be born again, he cannot see the kingdom of God"—showing plainly that without regeneration, or the new birth, there is no salvation.

We will only quote one more passage, Rom. iii. 10–23: "As it is written, There is none righteous, no, not one.   They are all gone out of the way,   and all the world may become guilty before God.   For all have sinned and come short of the glory of God." The apostle here proves that all, both Jews and Gentiles, are in the same depraved condition, and must be saved by faith in Jesus Christ.

The universality of wickedness, man's own consciousness of his natural tendency to sin, the general resistance of virtue that make watchfulness, education, influence, and conflicts necessary to counteract the force of evil, and the strong tendency of man to sin, sustained by the Bible, convince us man is depraved.

Neither Jesus, nor God through his word, ever commanded people to do impossibilities; and the command is for *all* to repent. Acts xvii. 30: "And the times of this ignorance God winked at; but now *commandeth all men everywhere to repent.*" It would be solemn mockery to command men to do that which they cannot do, or that which will do them no good. We will only refer to one more passage —Acts x. 43: "To him gave all the prophets witness, that through his name *whosoever* believeth in him shall receive remission of sins."

From our own conscience, from the usages and belief of all civilized nations, and from the teachings of the Scriptures, we are satisfied that salvation is free—that all can be saved if they desire, and will put their desires in practice.

As all men can be saved, we will now notice the condition on which they may be saved.

CHAPTER VII.

JUSTIFICATION.

TO be justified is to be absolved, or freed from guilt. Justification is pardon. When the Bible tells us how we are, or may be, justified, it simply means how we are pardoned, or forgiven. "We are accounted righteous before God, only for the merit of our Lord and Saviour Jesus Christ, by faith, and not for our own works or deservings; wherefore, that we are justified by faith only, is a most wholesome doctrine, and very full of comfort."

For a full exegesis of this subject we would refer the reader to Mr. Wesley's sermon on Justification, and Ralston's "Elements of Divinity."

Faith is the only condition of justification. We mean by this that we might have faith without anything else, and we be justified; we might have all things else, without faith, and we cannot be justified. There are some things that are prerequisite to faith, and there are some things that strengthen our faith. While faith is the act of the creature, it is also the gift of God.

Repentance is necessary to faith. We would

ness.   Now to him that *worketh* is the reward not
reckoned of grace, but of debt.   But to him that
worketh not, but *believeth* on him that justifieth the
ungodly, his *faith* is counted for righteousness.   For
we say that *faith* was reckoned unto Abraham for
righteousness."   We must notice when Abraham
had this faith: we learn from Rom. iv. 11, "And he
received the sign of circumcision, a seal of the righteousness of the *faith which he had, yet being uncir-
cumcised."*   We see he had this faith before he was
circumcised.   "For the promise, that he should be
the heir of the world, was not to Abraham, or to his
seed, through the law, but through the righteousness
of *faith."*   When St. James asks, "Was not Abraham, our father, justified by works when he offered
up his son Isaac?" he did not wish to convey the
idea that Abraham was never justified before that
time, for he had been, for twenty-four years (see
Gen. xv. 6), but wished to impress the Church that
faith would die if it were not exercised.   Faith will
produce works.

We can see how the Israelites were justified from
Rom. ix. 31, 32: "But Israel, which followed after
the law of righteousness, hath not attained to the
law of righteousness."   Wherefore? or why?   "Because they sought it not by faith, but as it were by
the works of the law."   This shows us that neither
their works of righteousness—such as sacrifices and

burnt-offerings—nor their obedience gave them pardon, but their *faith.*

We have proved from the New Testament that the Old Bible way of justifying was by faith. We will now notice only a few of the many passages in the New Testament that prove we are justified by faith only.

We will first cite the language of Christ—John i. 12, 13: "But as many as received him, to them gave he power to become the *sons of God,* even to them that *believe* on his name: which *were born,* not of blood, nor of the will of the flesh, nor of the will of man, but of God." If we are "sons," we are "heirs of God, and joint-heirs with Christ," having an inheritance in heaven, on the condition of our faith. This corresponds with 1 John v. 1: "Whosoever believeth that Jesus is the Christ is born of God." John xx. 31: "But these are written that ye might *believe* that Jesus is the Christ, the Son of God; and that believing ye might have life through his name." "Life," in this passage, is equivalent to justification, and is given on the condition of faith, or believing.

We shall next refer to the preaching of the apostles, first noticing that passage which has been so frequently misunderstood, thereby causing many to err. It is often misinterpreted in two respects— first, as to whom it is addressed, and, second, as to

amount of one hundred dollars, and have not the money to pay for them, and he agrees to take my note. I would write it thus:

$100 00. $100 00.
One day after date I promise to pay Mr. Smith one hundred dollars ($100 00) "for" value received.
Feb. 6, 1879.   (Signed)   —— ——.

At the expiration of six months Mr. Smith comes to me, and asks me for the money. I tell him I owe him nothing. He presents the note, and I claim it as my receipt, or claim that he owes me that amount. He asks me how it is, and I tell him that he misunderstands the note—that I claim that *for* means *in order that I*, or *in order to*, and he owes me $100.

We see, when we make Peter mean "Repent and be baptized *for*"—*in order to*—"the remission of sins," we cause him to convey a meaning different from that which he intended; but if we read it, "Repent and be baptized, for" your "*hearts have been purified*"—which is "the remission of sins"—there is some consistency; for to have the "heart purified by faith," and to "believe that Jesus is the Christ," must be regeneration, or pardon, or forgiveness, or "remission of sins." Peter did not promise them the forgiveness of sins, but "the gift of the Holy Ghost." As I give my note "*for value received,*" or *because I have received value*, so I am baptized "*for the remission of sins,*" or *because I have re-*

mission of sins. Baptism was the sign, or witness, to the *world* that we are Christians, or have received the remission of sins, and the "gift of the Holy Ghost" is the witness given to *us* to know that we are Christians. "The Spirit itself beareth witness with our spirit, that we are the children of God." Acts xi. 17: "Forasmuch, then, as God gave them the like gift" (of the Holy Ghost) "as he did unto us" (Jews, on the day of Pentecost), "who *believed* on the Lord Jesus Christ, what was I, that I could withstand God?" Peter used this language in defense for having preached to the Gentiles. By reference to Acts x. 43, we can see what he preached. He was sent for by Cornelius, who was a mourner, to hear what he must do to be saved, or to receive the remission of his sins. Cornelius was a Gentile, a sinner, although a penitent one. He had never been baptized. He prayed. God heard his prayers, and in answer to them Peter was sent for, and he went. He preached the gospel to the Gentiles— the life, death, and resurrection of Jesus. He said that "he" (Jesus) "commanded him to preach unto the people;" and here is what he was commanded to preach: "To him give all the prophets witness, that through his name whosoever believeth in him shall receive remission of sins." As Cornelius was an earnest, praying listener, he accepted the proposition at once, and believed; for "while Peter yet

fied from past sins, says it is by works, and then refers to the time Abraham was justified in offering Isaac, which was some twenty-four years after he "believed in the Lord, and he counted it to him for righteousness" (Gen. xv. 6); and nowhere in the Bible is it said that a man is justified from past sins by obedience. See and consider 1 Cor. i. 14.

CHAPTER VIII.

BAPTISM—ITS DESIGN.

A S we have proved in the preceding chapter that we are justified from past sins by faith only, and not by baptism, it now only remains for us to state the design of baptism.

Ralston says: "We arrive, then, at the conclusion that although water baptism should not be too lightly esteemed, and either set aside as not necessary under the gospel, or viewed as merely a form of initiation, or as a help to the exercise of faith, neither, on the other hand, should it be exalted too highly, as possessing intrinsic virtue and saving efficacy. The truth is this: it is a *sign* of a Christian man's profession, and also of the inward spiritual grace of regeneration and sanctification, and a *seal* of the gracious covenant by which the Church-relation and promises of eternal life are confirmed unto God's people."

THE MODE.—There has been so much said and written on this subject we will be very brief.

Baptism* is from the Greek βαπτιζω (*baptizo*),

---

* The Bible speaks of baptism under about eleven differ-

www.ingramcontent.com/pod-product-compliance
Lightning Source LLC
Chambersburg PA
CBHW032110010726
47493CB00008B/2533